Patience
and the
Porsche

also by
Valentina Sgro

Organize Your Family's Schedule...In No Time

Patience
and the
Porsche

Valentina Sgro

For Doran & Elias –
May all your
911s be Porsches!

Val
Sgro

GREEN SQUARE PUBLISHING
CLEVELAND

This book is a work of fiction.
Names, characters, businesses, organizations, places, events,
and incidents are the products of the author's imagination or are
used fictitiously. Any resemblance to actual events or locales or
persons, living or dead, is entirely coincidental.

© 2007 Valentina Sgro
All rights reserved

Illustrations by Carl E. Cormany

Manufactured in the United States of America
Printed on acid-free paper

ISBN-10: 0-9793552-0-6
ISBN-13: 978-0-9793552-0-2

Library of Congress Control Number: 2007922884

Quantity discounts are available on bulk purchases of this book
for educational or promotional purposes. Special books or book
excerpts can also be created to fit specific needs.
For infomation, please contact the publisher.

Published by
Green Square Publishing
www.greensquarepublishing.com

FIRST EDITION
First printing
2007

this book is dedicated to

my father

who encouraged me to write fiction

Chapter 1

Pat turned to look back into the living room as she always did as she left for work. Her eyes noted the collection of shoes sitting just inside the door, skimmed briefly over the wilted plant in the corner, and rested for a moment on the remains of her light breakfast – a half-empty teacup and a plate of cookie crumbs – on the dining room table that was just visible beyond the living room. Her mind's eye noted regretfully the eggshells that should have been sent down the garbage disposal still sitting in the kitchen sink and the jumble of recipes she had left sitting out on the counter. Then Pat turned, pulled the door shut behind her, jiggled the knob to make sure it had locked, and headed toward the garage. And she concluded her departure preparations with her usual thought: *Why am I going out to organize someone else when I should be staying home and organizing myself?*

Patience "Pat" (no middle name) Oaktree, was a professional organizer. She helped her clients, from a wide variety of backgrounds and situations, get organized through tailored combinations of de-cluttering and time management. And she prided herself on developing innovative systems that would allow her clients to stay organized even after Pat was no longer on site. Each situation was unique and the circumstances were quite challenging, considering that most people did not seek out professional organizing services until they were close to des-perate. Pat and her organizing colleagues across the country were confident that one day organizing would be a more mainstream profession and people would mention their professional organizer – or PO – the same way they referred to their CPA, MD, and lawyer. But that day was a way off.

In the meantime, Pat was still glad she had

stumbled into the profession. And she liked the fact that her initials were PO. She had played around with all sorts of names for her business that would highlight this coincidence. Names like Pleasing Order or Practically Organized. Then she would have a triple "PO" and could write a jingle that went "po-po-po!" But in one sense it was too cute – sort of like Santa Claus meets professional organizing. And in another sense it was just plain stupid. Then she thought of Patience Oaktree, Organizing Professional – but that came out as POOP, which would not do at all!

Next, she had tried capitalizing on her somewhat unusual first name. Perhaps a tagline like: Let Patience be your guide. And she had spent days playing around in her mind with similar slogans. In the end, she determined that her lack of satisfaction would not keep her from exercising her entre-preneurial spirit, and Pat launched her business simply as Patience Oaktree, Professional Organizer – jingles, taglines, and slogans to follow.

Now, eight years later, Pat, by her own humble assessment, was the most successful professional organizer in the State. She had started out primarily with an absolute passion for helping others. Having read almost every book in print on the subject in an effort to get herself organized, Pat was convinced that most of them were of little use. They told disorganized people about the organizing systems and tools that worked for organized people. These were not the systems and tools that work for people who are not naturally organized to begin with. Pat had been absolutely right about that. But that's where the accuracy of her evaluation stopped. Pat had wrongly concluded that the system that worked for Pat – which was different from all of the published born-organized solutions – would work for everyone else who needed organizing help. Fortunately for her future success, Pat was a woman of the late Twentieth Century, endeavoring not to be left behind by the Twenty-First Century, and therefore she was what society now terms a lifelong learner. Along with the passion for her new profession came a commitment to learn everything about the field. Pat joined the two leading professional associations, attended seminars, read the cutting-edge literature, and learned a whole bunch. Now, she could tell within ten minutes whether she would enjoy working with a prospective client and, within an hour, she could analyze whether her skills would serve the client's needs. If these two criteria weren't met, Pat would refer the person to one of her colleagues who Pat felt would be a better match. As a result, Pat liked the clients she worked with and had a near-perfect customer satisfaction record. If that wasn't success, Pat didn't know what was!

Still, always nagging at the back of Pat's mind was the fact that she was not turning the kind of profit she had envisioned and that she still believed possible. Indeed, it was her frustration with this monetary shortfall that had subconsciously prodded her to take on the client she was on her way to see. It was an interesting case that flew in the face of several business rules that Pat had written for herself over the years. If she were honest with herself, she had agreed to help this client mostly out of greed. Yes, this one was to be all about improving the bottom line.

Chapter 2

So, here was Pat headed off to meet with her new client for the first time. That already broke Pat's first rule, which was to never take on a client until she had met with them in person. As a result, instead of the slight anxiety and general exhilaration she usually felt, Pat was on her way with a rather worrisome sense of trepidation.

Pat had been sitting at her desk in her office – a converted spare bedroom – contemplating once again the book she hoped to write, the book which had been at the top of her New Year's Resolutions list for three years running, when the call came in.

"Hello, this is Pat."

Silence … then, "Is this Patience Oaktree, Professional Organizer?"

"Yes, this is Pat."

"May I speak with Patience?"

To herself Pat said, *Patience, Patience.* Indeed, in eight years Pat never had developed a catchy slogan playing on the use of her first name. But, over the years she had frequently admonished herself with the phrase "Patience, Patience," the first use of the word being a directive and the second being her name. It had become a sort of silent mantra.

Aloud, she responded, "This is Patience. Pat." She reminded herself to leave any impatience out of her tone, and managed, almost. While this could be an annoying telemarketer, it also could be a newspaper reporter or prospective client. One never knew and must keep an open mind so as not to be off-putting to a person prepared to offer a rewarding opportunity.

The uncertain voice at the other end continued, "Well, yes, you see, I need to hire an organizer."

"That's what we're here for," encouraged Pat, who tried her best to sound perky and interested. "Why don't you tell me a little about your situation?"

"Well, you see, I've always been a mess, and my sister hates it. I can't fit another thing in my closets, there's stuff all over, it's just a mess! Can you help?"

"Most likely, but please tell me a little more. You mentioned your sister. Does she live with you? What makes now the time you've decided to get organized?"

"Well, you see, no, my sister doesn't live with me. She's quite well off and doesn't think I'm ever going to amount to anything. She hates the way I live. She's issued me a challenge because she thinks I can't do it. She's a psychologist and thinks she knows everything. You see, I want to prove her wrong and get the money."

And then the absolutely unique proposition unfolded. This woman's sister – very self-righteous, thought Pat – had told her that if she could get her house organized and keep it that way for six months, the sister would give her $100,000. This woman wanted to hire Pat on a contingency-fee basis without the sister knowing. If Pat helped her meet the challenge, she would pay Pat $25,000 out of the $100,000 from her sister.

Pat had never heard of such a thing, but she kept her cool. "Wow, that's really interesting … I'm sorry, I didn't catch your name."

"Susan."

"Susan. Thanks. My first thought is that this would be a project that would take quite a bit of time."

"Well, you see, I get three weeks vacation, and I could take it all at once so we could get a good solid start. Can you help me?"

Red flags were popping up around every thought Pat was having. Susan was being motivated at worst by anger and spite and at best by money, not an interest in improving her life. Red flag! Susan had a hesitancy to be totally open with Pat; she still hadn't revealed her last name or where she lived. Red flag! Susan was not above deceit, seeing as she didn't want her sister to know she had enlisted Pat's help. Red flag! Pat's payment was deferred and not guaranteed. Big red flag!

And yet Pat could feel herself being sucked in as if she were standing on the beach with her toes just at the edge of the water while a strong undertow pulled out the sand from under them.

I must buy time to think this through. "I'll have to see if I can clear three weeks on my calendar. Would it be okay if I call you back this afternoon?" And Pat proceeded adeptly to elicit Susan's phone number and the street and city where she lived.

"And your sister's name?"

"Helen Huffman, Ph.D." That had been almost too easy, thought Pat. Said with contempt, apparently Susan didn't care about her sister's privacy. Another red flag?

As soon as she hung up the phone, Pat began her research. It was scary the amount of investigative information one had at one's fingertips these days. She cross-checked the phone number Susan had given her with the phone number that showed on the caller-ID. It matched. She plugged the number into the reverse look-up feature of the free online phone book, got lucky, and found Susan's address and full name. Susan Huffman. One could not have assumed it, but no surprise there. Pat then Googled Susan and learned that she had a degree in management from the local state university and currently worked as a bank branch manager. Pat knew from a former bank manager client that this meant that

Susan was responsible for increasing the amount of money deposited by customers at her branch. Her job was dependent on her ability to bring in new money and, these days, was tenuous at best.

Pat also checked out Susan's sister, the psychologist. It turned out her first name was Hellen, with two *l*s, which made her easier to distinguish. She had extensive credentials, including several research grants, and lived in an outlying suburb where Pat knew the minimum lot size was five acres. Pat noted that Hellen's research was in areas that did not impact one's ability to organize – no research in ADD (attention deficit disorder), OCD (obsessive-compulsive disorder), hoarding, TBI (traumatic brain injury), or even cognition. So, thought Pat, maybe Dr. Know-it-all doesn't know much when it comes to overcoming chronic disorganization. Still, Pat was a little jealous since she had thought many times how great it would be to receive grant money to look into any number of areas having to do with organizing. But then that would require her to get herself organized enough to actually apply for a grant.

What had Pat concluded from her sleuthing? Not

much. She had confirmed what she had been told. She already knew that Susan and Hellen were in different economic brackets and didn't get along. On the downside, she could be reasonably sure that Susan could not pay her $25,000 unless she won the challenge money from her sister. On the upside, she could be reasonably sure that the sister had not issued the challenge based on any expert knowledge that Susan had a psychological condition that would prevent her from succeeding, and she could be reasonably confident that the sister had the money if she chose to pay it.

Still, all in all, Pat knew that taking this client was a big gamble. But the lure of the big bucks had hooked her. And even though Susan's success would be dependent on Susan being motivated, Pat was hopeful that the fact that Susan would keep three quarters of the money would be motivation enough. It should be, even if Susan were only as greedy as Pat. Pat did not want to be greedy, so she asked herself if it were not possible that she was being driven by a more noble purpose, perhaps the intellectual challenge of an interesting case or the desire to help Susan change habits that were negatively impacting her life.

As Pat drove along, she realized that motive was now a moot point. Whatever had gripped her that day, she had accepted the assignment sight unseen. And now, on this Monday in January, it would be only moments before Susan's house would come into view.

Chapter 3

The drive from Pat's house to Susan's took only about fifteen minutes. In that time Pat passed through several communities. Pat herself lived in what she viewed as an older suburb where many of the houses were approaching the century mark. They were medium- to large-size homes with many rooms and very small closets. Susan lived a little farther from the City, in what Pat considered a middle-aged suburb, many of the houses having been built in the boom of the 1960s with relatively open floor plans and little charm. Farther still from the City were the newer suburbs such as the one in which Dr. Hellen lived, where the houses had oversized rooms and closets as big as the bedrooms in Pat's neighborhood. Each suburb with its own style, and each with its own distinctive organizing challenges.

Pat checked her computer-generated directions and turned onto Susan's street. The houses were not quite as Pat had envisioned, but were small- and medium-sized bungalows, some a story and a half and some a full two stories. Most of them had detached one-car garages, which indicated to Pat that these homes were probably built earlier than the rest of the suburb, shortly after World War II, not in the 60s when automobiles and garages became a more integral part of life. It was hard to be sure, given the snowpack, but Pat had the impression that these homes were well maintained. Many of the driveways had been neatly shoveled. An elderly man in one yard was busy filling his bird feeders. A woman two doors farther down was dragging a Christmas tree out to the curb, its few remaining strands of tinsel flapping and glinting.

Pat turned into Susan's driveway. It had been shoveled at some time, but the latest snowfall was merely packed down from numerous tire passes. A fairly weathered sedan – Pat guessed it was Susan's – was parked outside the closed garage door – a good indication that the garage was too full of other things to contain its intended inhabitant. The bungalow itself looked rather small, and Pat thought that it must be pretty bad inside if Susan thought it would take weeks to organize. *Don't be judgmental!* Perhaps Susan, unlike most clients, was a realist and understood that a mess that took years to get into could not be gotten out of overnight. The recent popularity of cable TV shows featuring home clean-ups had only fueled that popular misconception. How many times had Pat had to tell people that to accomplish what happened on TV in thirty minutes would take a crew of ten people two weeks, to the tune of about $20,000? It seemed nobody really wanted to hear the reality of reality television.

A large picture window was the primary architectural feature of the house's front. It was mostly obscured, though, by two overgrown bushes. They looked like juniper plants, a poor choice for anyone who didn't want the seasonal job of trimming them back. From an efficiency point of view, slower growing, more shapely shrubs would be better. Only the top six inches of the front door were visible – it, too, was hidden by bushes that at one time no doubt had been intended to give it a welcoming attitude but now seemed to serve more like a no trespassing sign. The second floor windows were still visible, but all of their shades were drawn. Pat's initial assessment – the accuracy of which she would soon learn from Susan – was that this unwelcoming appearance was the outward reflection of Susan's reluctance to let anyone into her very cluttered home.

Pat pulled a green 3x5 index card from her briefcase and quickly scrawled the heading "Outdoor Organizing Book" followed by the sentence: If yard work is not something you enjoy, don't plant fast-growing shrubs (ex. juniper) near your front door or under picture windows. She scanned what she had written and after the word "enjoy" inserted "and you don't have a gardener." Then she tucked the card into the briefcase pocket; when she got home – or, more realistically, the next time she decided to clean out her briefcase – Pat would toss the card into her book idea box, where it would stay until she actually got around to writing her book someday.

Pat turned her attention back to her assessment of Susan's house and looked over to compare it to the neighbors'. There, in the next-door driveway to the north was a shiny, iconic, black Porsche 911. In an instant, several thoughts flashed through Pat's mind:

How out of place! In a modest neighborhood such as this, Pat would not expect anyone to own a Porsche. Maybe in Dr. Hellen's neighborhood, but not here. Perhaps it was owned by an eccentric who spent all his money on his car and didn't have anything left over for an opulent house. *What an imagination you have, Pat!*

How odd that Porsche hasn't changed the name of this model! Pat had dated a car buff back in her college days, so she knew that the 911 had been around for at least thirty years. But it still seemed odd after the terrorist attacks of September 11, 2001, that this would be the name of a sports car. Then again, maybe it was a sign that we really weren't letting the terrorists run our lives and that 911 could still have a positive connotation for some people.

Pat's reverie about the existence of this particular

automobile and its kind in general was interrupted by the emergence from the neighbor's side door of the apparent owner of the vehicle. A man in his early thirties, Pat would guess, impeccably and expensively dressed. Now, Pat was no fashionista and wouldn't know an Armani from a Hickey-Freeman. In fact, Pat had once bought a pair of Armani socks on a trip to Milan, Italy, just to feel she had been part of the fashion scene without breaking the bank. Eleven euros for a pair of socks was a lot, but at least Pat could afford them; she could not fathom 9,000 euros for the Prada carry-on bag she had seen, with plastic handles! Woven into the black socks were pretty little pink and blue color bursts that matched one of Pat's suits. Later, when Pat's fashion-aware cousin saw the socks, she had remarked, "Oh, how nice, the Armani eagle!" Pat hadn't even known that the Armani trademark was an eagle. Still, Pat could tell an expensive suit from the department store variety, and the man in Susan's neighbor's driveway was definitely wearing an expensive suit.

He also had a great physique, elegant features, and beautiful chestnut curls, the kind that didn't have a strand out of place and yet looked totally natural. Pat wondered if they would still look that way on a sunny spring day as this man drove along the freeway with the top down? Now, Pat herself was married – very happily for the past twenty-two years. Still, she could appreciate from a distance a young, handsome man in a Porsche.

In the thirty seconds it took for all of these thoughts to skip through Pat's mind, Mr. Rich Gorgeous, as she had nicknamed him in her head, hopped into his sports car, started the engine, waved to someone unseen in the house, and zipped off down the street.

Pat, reluctantly but quickly, refocused her attention on Susan's house. She took a deep breath, reminded herself that she must now assess the client and the house without sounding at all judgmental, and that she must articulate the appropriate organizing knowledge in a professional but friendly way so that she could begin building the trust and confidence of her new client. Pat considered herself a very genuine person. Still, she always reminded herself as she approached a client's place that, if all else failed, she must pretend she was on stage and not break character with strange faces or errant sighs of frustration. Pat grabbed her case, locked the doors to her minivan, and rang the doorbell. It was, as she liked to call it, Showtime.

Chapter 4

Kkrrrriiiiiinnng! Pat could hear the sound of the old-fashioned doorbell as she pushed the button. The sound gave Pat confidence in her impression that this home was built before the 1950s. The sound was so different from the classic singsongy "ding-dong" of the 50s bells that had been imprinted on people's minds with the commercial phrase "Avon calling!"

After a few seconds, the bolt turned and the door opened.

"Hi! I'm Pat Oaktree." Pat extended her hand. "You must be Susan." And keeping her cheery smile of greeting on her face, Pat's brain with computer-like speed and accuracy sized up her new client. Late twenties or early thirties – but looks could be so deceiving. About five-foot-four, not overweight or underweight – a good sign that disorganization hadn't led to bad eating habits. Dressed in blue jeans and a plain light blue sweatshirt with her shoulder-length, strawberry blonde hair pulled back in a ponytail – either trying to give an air of ease or ready to get down to serious de-cluttering. Oh, bunny slippers on the feet! Make that definitely an air of ease.

Pat stepped into the small entryway, made even tighter by a hall tree bulky from its many layers of jackets, coats, hats, and umbrellas, rather like an indoor version of the overgrown shrubbery outside.

"Yes, I'm Susan. Thank you so much for coming. I hope you don't run away after you see the place."

"Of course not! Let's start by getting a little better acquainted. Is there someplace we can sit and talk?"

"We can try the kitchen. But, no, you see the breakfast dishes are still on the table. Let's try the living room, but you'll have to move some newspapers in order to sit down."

Once Pat got past the hall tree she saw that the

living room opened straight off the entryway. It was not large, but, of course, it looked tiny with all the books, papers, boxes, exercise devices, and other stuff spread around. Still, it was easy enough to spot the couch, remove a small pile, and have a seat. Susan sat herself down in a rocking chair, and Pat suspected the rocking motion was helping Susan relieve some stress.

"You see, I don't know where to start." Susan spoke in a flat voice, and Pat somehow knew that this was a line Susan had memorized ahead of time.

"We should start with a plan," asserted Pat. "Start by telling me why it is that you want to change things from the way they are."

"I want to show that stuck-up sister of mine that she's wrong about me!"

"That's understandable. But, tell me the truth, if it weren't for your sister's attitude, would you be perfectly content to keep things just the way they are?"

Susan's eyes became glassy. She rocked a little faster. Then she burst into tears and practically shouted, "I hate it, I hate it, I hate it! I hate that I have to watch where I step so I don't twist my ankle! I hate that I can never find what I'm looking for, and when I do it's usually ruined! I hate that my sister is right that I'm a mess! That I can't have friends over! That when I come home after work this place just sucks all the energy out of me! It's hopeless!"

Oh crud! thought Pat. I didn't want the dam to break so soon into our conversation, we haven't even built any rapport yet, and now she's going to feel even more embarrassed. I totally misjudged her level of anxiety. Now I'm going to have to do damage control.

"It's okay. I know this is a stressful situation to be in, and that maybe your sister pushed you to call me a little before you were ready. But, it's really a good thing that you feel this way, because now that I know you have some self-motivation I'm much more confident that I'll be able to help you achieve some success." *Whoa, sometimes I can be pretty eloquent on the fly.*

Pat looked around for a tissue box but didn't spot one. So she reached into her case and pulled out a packet of her own. "Here, finish up that good cry, release that tension. Then we can focus on a workable plan."

A few minutes and the entire packet of tissues

later, as Susan's sobs subsided, Pat continued, "So, I heard you mention a couple of real goals: to be able to walk around freely, to be able to invite people over without embarrassment – or a mad cleaning frenzy. And to be able to find things and keep them in good condition. And your vision is that those things will make your house a home, a haven, a place you'll want to be. Have I got it right?"

"I guess so. You see, I don't think it's possible."

***

Pat accompanied Susan on a tour of the house. Pat, being a very visual learner, was trying to take in all the clues she could possibly see. There was the surface clutter, the sub-layers of disorganization, and, underneath it all, the original structure that had obviously not worked as Susan had at one time intended. At the same time, knowing she was not an auditory learner – how often had she forgotten someone's name within five seconds of being introduced! – Pat was struggling to listen to Susan's banter as they went along. Pat knew she had already made one big mistake with Susan and was anxious not to make another during their first meeting.

The house, it turned out, was one and a half

stories, and Susan's bedroom was a corner room at the front of the house on the second floor. As Pat had noted from her car, the window shades and draperies were drawn tight.

Pat noticed immediately that the double bed had a double personality. Half of the bed, on the side farthest from the bedroom door, was piled head to foot about three feet high with several stacks. Nearest the headboard – a beautiful honey oak with modern, easy-to-dust lines – was a mound of towels, sheets, and blankets. Toward the middle, papers of varying sorts cascaded – newspapers, magazines, envelopes and packets that looked like unopened mail, and file folders with their contents oozing out. At the foot of the bed were clothes. They looked like they had been, in the first instance, placed deliberately. Out of the bottom of the stack, with legs draped to hang unwrinkled over the edge of the bed, were a pair of brown wool slacks and a pair of khakis. Various cloth arms and legs stuck out elsewhere from what had become, over time, an entangled heap. Under all of this stuff on the far side of the bed were the neatly flat layers of the made bed – a yellow bedspread, an orange blanket, and crisp yellow sheets with little orange flowers.

The close side of the bed had been slept in and was not made. The covers flung back as Susan had exited the bed, the crumpled pillow and flowered bottom sheet lay exposed with a rumple of top sheet, the blanket and spread loose except where they were secured along the foot of the bed. The movement of these layers looked like it could have been responsible for some of the avalanching of papers on the far side.

Under the bed, Pat could see lots of books and dust.

Susan had not yet mentioned the bed, but was busily describing other areas of the bedroom.

"You see, here is the pile where I put everything that needs to go to the dry cleaners. Oh! There's the purple blouse I wanted to wear to our staff meeting last week, but couldn't find – I guess I didn't realize how long it's been since I've taken anything to the cleaners.

"And here's my hamper for dirty laundry."

"There's a lot piled on top of it. How often do you do your laundry?"

"Well, you see, I try to do it every week. And

mostly I do. You see, there's nothing in the hamper," Susan lifted the lid partway to prove her point, "so I don't have as many dirty clothes as you thought.

"And here, you see, are my clean clothes from last week." Susan waved her hand proudly at three laundry baskets lined up at the foot of the bed. Pat could identify a separate load of laundry in each basket. All of the clothes had been neatly folded except for the basket of underwear.

Putting two and two together, Pat identified the strata on a nearby chair. "And those, I'm guessing, would be the clothes left from the past couple of weeks' laundry?" From bottom to top, they both could see two pairs of folded jeans, several t-shirts, a couple more pairs of slacks, some more shirts, and a crown of underwear.

"Oh, yes! I guess you've figured out that I put my clean clothes there when I need to empty the laundry baskets for the next load," said Susan as if she was pleased that she actually had a system.

"And how about the dresser drawers and closet? Are they empty like the hamper?"

"Oh, no! They're full, you see. And all my clothes fit me," Susan added triumphantly. Pat was disappointed, as she always liked finding empty cabinets, drawers, and boxes, and she had been hopeful here based on the state of the hamper. On the other hand, Pat was glad that Susan was showing some enthusiasm and hadn't picked up on Pat's disappointment.

Pat turned the closet knob and, shielding herself behind the door, slowly opened it. There wasn't much air in the closet, but nothing fell out. Next she reached for a drawer pull. She had to squeeze her other hand in between the drawer and its frame and push down hard on the contents in order to pull the drawer open. Released from the tension, a springy group of t-shirts popped up as if to say, "wear me! wear me!" They could not be coaxed back, and Pat and Susan left the room with the liberated t-shirts still basking in the air of freedom.

Across the hall was Susan's bathroom, a jumble of personal care and beauty products. *An organizing project in itself.*

The only other room on the upper half-floor was a storage closet. Susan explained that it contained decorations for various holidays, old paperwork, memorabilia, and assorted other items she "might find a use for someday." When Pat asked her to elaborate, Susan admitted that the decorations were buried too deep to reach and that she really hadn't even opened the door in three years as there wasn't a cubic inch of space in which to store anything else. Pat insisted, kindly but firmly, that they take a look inside. There was a light bulb with a pull switch just inside the door, but, when Pat pulled on the chain, nothing happened.

"Oh, the bulb must have burnt out! I'll get a new one," said Susan, opening the linen cabinet in the bathroom. She extracted a fluorescent tube for the bathroom fixture and a packet of tiny nightlight bulbs, but no 60-watt bulb. Before Pat could stop her, Susan was on her way down the steps to the kitchen. So Pat followed. Susan rummaged through three different drawers and produced two new packets of chandelier bulbs. "You see, I don't use this pearlescent kind any more." Then she was off to the basement. Again, Pat followed. The "tool room" contained a case of three-way bulbs and a couple loose Christmas lights.

"I guess I don't have any regular bulbs," concluded Susan with a small sigh of defeat.

"That's okay. We can just continue our house tour from here in the basement," encouraged Pat, as she jotted herself a note to make sure to help Susan set up designated areas for each type of supply so that she could determine her current inventory at a moment's glance, rather than after a ten-minute search.

The basement had a laundry room that also housed the furnace and hot-water tank. As Susan had suggested, the laundry situation looked in pretty good order. A few rumpled shirts hung on a rack near the ironing board. Pat's quick peeks into the washer and dryer did not reveal any stagnant or, worse yet, mildewing loads. There were the corners filled with piles of dryer fabric softener sheets, but those should be easy enough to deal with. And then, then there was what Pat instantly dubbed in her own head "The Wall of Food." *Oops, better be careful not to be judgmental.*

"I see you've installed some shelves so you can use this room as a pantry," commented Pat, hoping to initiate a discussion. Susan did not let her down.

"Yes, you see, I just didn't have room in the kitchen for all of the food," Susan replied logically.

"Do you entertain a lot?"

"No, not really," Susan said innocently. But then she quickly caught on to Pat's drift. "I like to take advantage of sales, you see ... and to be prepared in case of an emergency." Pat detected a dose of self-satisfaction, along with a hint of defensiveness.

"Well, I haven't seen your kitchen yet, so I can't have an opinion as to whether this is the ideal system for you," Pat diffused. "But, I just have to ask about this huge plastic container of pasta." Pat didn't need to gesture to the five-gallon food storage container that was not quite, but almost, full of elbow macaroni.

"That's from the macaroni and cheese boxes." And then, in response to Pat's quizzical look, "I love the cheese sauce that comes in the packages, but I prefer whole wheat macaroni. So I've been saving the ones from the boxes, because you can't just waste it, can you, with people starving? I'm going to donate it to the food bank."

Pat was sure there was something wrong with the logic. Would the food bank take unwrapped pasta? (Probably.) Just how old was the oldest elbow at the bottom? (Pasta has a virtually unlimited shelf life.)

Was Susan going to give it away in the relatively expensive container? Did that matter? But, Pat really had no good reply at the moment.

And so the tour continued.

The kitchen contained every tool a chef could dream of owning. A complete set of copper-bottomed pots and pans – "The whole set cost less than the five pieces I wanted if I bought them separately." A pasta maker, a bread maker, a juicer, a countertop electric hibachi, an espresso maker, and a Belgian waffle iron – "They were having a countertop appliance super-sale on the shopping network one night when I was up late working on expense reports, you see." Two each of three sizes of cake pan, two pie pans, regular muffin tins, mini-muffin tins, loaf pans, cookie sheets, a bundt cake pan, a springform pan, large ramekins, small ramekins, ladyfinger molds, and more – "Lots of my friends invite me to baking club home parties, and I don't think it's polite to go and not buy anything." A drawer full of measuring cups, measuring spoons, frosting spreaders, spatulas and whisks of all sizes, an apple corer, a watermelon boat carver, and more – "Those are the hostess gifts from when I had my own baking club party." A similar assortment of plastic food storage containers, with a similar explanation.

The upper cabinets contained five complete sets of dishes. "My grandmother's china, my mother's china, my yard-sale steal-of-a-deal set from college, my first new set with the cups that don't fit in the dishwasher," Susan ticked them off from left to right across the top shelf; then pointing to the ones on the lower shelf, "The set I use."

One of the bottom cabinets was crammed full of cookbooks.

Upon a quick look at the larger of the two bedrooms on the first floor, Pat saw a double bed piled high with papers, a stair machine, a weight machine, a dresser with what looked like a sweatshirt sticking out of a partially opened drawer, a television, and a corner filled with an old computer, peripherals, and cables. The closet contained a vacuum cleaner surrounded by a jumble of papers, books, and bed linens. There was not much room to walk.

The smaller bedroom was lined with shelves containing books, stacks of magazines, knickknacks, cleaning supplies, a few pots with some plant remains, and movie videos. There also was a working computer. Two chairs and the floor were covered with boxes and bags, the contents of which would, at this point in time, remain a mystery to Pat.

Pat had already seen the living room-dining room "L" during Susan's untimely crying jag. There was a very elegant mahogany dining room set – table, chairs, sideboard, and hutch – largely obscured by mounds of paper.

All that was left to complete the initial assessment was the garage. "Oh, I think I'm still too embarrassed to let you see it," began Susan. But, even as she spoke she led Pat back through the kitchen, with the breakfast dishes still on the table, to the door out to the attached one-and-a-half car garage.

The garage had that familiar garage smell, a mixture of gasoline, oil, burnt charcoal, and fertilizer. *Our sense of smell is often overlooked in the organizing process. There's an idea for one of my books!*

A lawn mower, a shelf filled with paint cans, another with flower pots, two lidless boxes containing a full aquarium setup complete with clay sunken pirate boat. Really pretty typical stuff.

"That's a great desk!" Pat seized upon a positive comment as she noticed that Susan's posture seemed to have slumped. And indeed, smack in the middle of the car stall was a superb medium-sized rolltop desk.

"Isn't it, though!" Susan beamed with pride and, Pat thought, relief. "I got it at a garage sale for only a hundred dollars!" Then she added, "But, you see, I couldn't get it into the house." Pat wondered if Susan meant the desk was too bulky and heavy to wrestle in, or if she meant that there was no room for it amidst all the clutter. Pat decided the more prudent course was not to ask. *What if my parents had named me Prudence? Then I could say to myself, "Prudence, Prudence" in situations like this. But "Patience, Patience" does have wider application.*

"Great," Pat summed up. "Is that everything? You didn't forget to show me or tell me about other stuff, did you? Perhaps a self-storage locker?"

"Oh no! This is it, except my office at work, which really isn't a problem."

"Nothing stashed in the trunk of your car, either?"

"Gosh, you're good! I forgot, you see, but how did

you know?"

That's why I'm the most successful organizer in the State.

"Remember I told you I couldn't get to my holiday decorations under the rafters upstairs? So, for Christmas I bought a beautiful new tree. You see, I thought about getting a real one for a change, but I was afraid I might start a fire. Then I saw this really good-looking one on sale, so I knew that was the way to go. But, after I called you, you see, I knew I would never open the door for you if my Christmas tree was still up. And then I thought how it fit in the trunk when I brought it home, so it seemed like a great place to put it. Temporarily, of course."

"Mmm." Pat had a suspicion that there might be other unrevealed stashes, but she let it go. Looking at her watch in an obvious and deliberate way – although she had snuck a peek ten minutes ago and knew exactly what time it was – Pat announced, "Twelve-ten, time for a lunch break. I need to run a couple errands, but I'll be back at one. Be sure to eat something to keep your energy up."

Pat made her way back through the kitchen with the breakfast dishes still on the table, through the living room with its books, papers, boxes, and exercise devices, past the overloaded hall tree, through the thicket of overgrown shrubs, into the invigorating January air, and then into her own personal space inside her minivan. *Aahh!*

Chapter 5

Pat loved her career, she really did. Being the most successful professional organizer in the State was very satisfying. But working with clients, while exhilarating, was also exhausting. And, she thought, even though she hadn't lost a pound since she opened her business eight years ago, it must burn a lot of calories, because working with clients made her hungry. Her clients would get tired and hungry, too. So Pat made sure they both always took a break every couple of hours.

Pat liked to get away at lunchtime and clear her head. Sometimes clients would insist they have lunch together, and Pat would charge for that time, but the money wasn't worth the sacrifice of a few minutes to decompress and recharge.

Pat pulled out of Susan's driveway and made her way back up the street, past the lady's tree lawn with its discarded Christmas tree – no artificial tree storage problems here – and past the bird feeder's yard where sparrows and cardinals were dining together harmoniously. Once on the main street, Pat pulled into the shopping center lot and parked the van. Then she pulled out her bagged lunch – a peanut butter and jelly sandwich, a banana, a snack size candy bar (because she had to have her chocolate) and a bottle of water.

Pat had settled on this combination as her standard packed lunch for several reasons. It was easy to make and, if she had to eat it with the client, it was something the client would neither be envious of nor repulsed by. (These days there was the slight concern that a client would have a severe peanut allergy and go into anaphylactic shock when Pat bit into the sandwich. She would have to remember to ask first.) Or, if the client insisted on feeding Pat, the sandwich wouldn't spoil. And likewise, it would keep if Pat were having one of those particularly trying days when she was forced to succumb to the comfort of a cheeseburger and fries at lunch in order to maintain a pleasant attitude through to the end of the work day. Three cheeseburger days in a row with the same client was the litmus test for determining that Pat and the client should not continue working together.

As Pat chewed literally on her lunch, she chewed figuratively on her analysis of Susan's organizing project. There was so much to be done that there were many different ways to approach it. Should Pat decide which method to use? Or should she present options to Susan and let her choose? Sometimes Pat wished she weren't so good an organizer; then she wouldn't think everything was as complicated as it really was. Ignorance could be bliss. *Stop overthinking things, Patience.* Pat would stick with the basics and build from there.

With fifteen minutes left on her break, Pat finished her candy bar and pulled out her cell phone and pressed speed dial number two.

The call went through and she heard the familiar greeting, "This is Frederic Watson."

"Hi, Fred. I just thought I'd give you a call before I go back to my new client's after lunch."

"How'd it go this morning?" her husband responded. Fred was an editor/artist for a medium-sized local publishing house. Someday, if she ever got around to writing them, Fred would edit and illustrate Pat's books.

"Pretty typical. A lot to do. But no animals, no apparent rodents or insects. No apparent mental disorder."

"Well, at least if the money doesn't pan out, it won't have been hell."

"Yeah, but I'm not running a charity, remember?"

"Sure, Pat, and no matter what, I know you'll do your usual great job. What time will you get home?"

"By six for sure. I'm only about fifteen minutes away, maybe twenty during rush hour. I'm cooking chicken for dinner."

"Sounds good. I'll be home around six-thirty. Love you."

"Love you, too. Bye."

"Bye. Ppch." Fred threw her a kiss, as he always did, before he clicked off.

Pat flipped her phone off, dropped it back into her

case, and was about to drive off when she noticed a hardware store in the shopping center where she had parked. Thinking back to Susan's bathroom, which they had not even discussed, Pat popped out of her car and made a quick acquisition before returning past the house with the now empty bird feeders and around the Christmas tree which had blown out into the street, to beat her way through the overgrown junipers back to Susan's door. Showtime, Act II!

Kkrrrriiiiiinnng! Pat waited. No answer.

Kkrrrriiiiiinnng! Still no answer. Pat looked around. Susan's car was in the driveway. There were no foot tracks in the snow. Susan had not left.

Kkrrrriiiiiinnng! The door flew open. "Sorry, you see, I just thought that a pot of tea would be nice. Would you like a cup? It's ready now."

"Lovely. Thank you." Pat followed Susan into the kitchen. The breakfast dishes were gone and a full tea service was laid out. Pat hoped that Susan's idea of tea was not an herbal infusion. She was not disappointed. It was a robust Darjeeling, full of taste and caffeine, just the sort of tea Pat would have fixed for herself had she been at home writing one of her books. Yes, Pat knew that this whole tea ritual was a stall tactic by Susan, and she knew that they would need another break in a couple of hours and tea would have been perfect then. But still, this really worked out quite well. They would form the organizing plan over a civilized pot of tea. Perhaps this would become a daily habit, evaluating and regrouping after lunch with a warming, comforting, energizing cup of tea. *Aahh.*

The tea poured, Pat dove into the matter at hand before Susan could divert the conversation. Lovely as the tea was, there was work to be done. The goal of having the house ready for Dr. Hellen's inspection in three weeks could be met, but only with diligent effort. Susan was ready.

"Well, then," Pat sounded like the authority she was, "the first step is for us to map out, to focus, if you will, the vision. We'll make a sheet with three columns for every room. In the first column we'll list the things that are in the room that you want to stay in the room. The second column will be things to move into the room. The third column will be things to move out of the room. We'll start as we sit here sipping our tea. We'll probably need to actually go stand in each room to complete the job."

Susan had thought that the larger bedroom on the first floor would be a guest room and the smaller bedroom would be an office.

"How often do you have houseguests?"

"Well, you see, I've never had a houseguest in the three years I've lived here ... what with the mess and all."

"Okay. We're talking about vision here. So, who would you envision your houseguests to be once everything is in good order?"

"Oh ... maybe my good friend who moved out of town."

"That would be a single house guest, or her whole family?"

"No, she's single."

"Then why not consider making the smaller room the guest room and the larger one your office?"

"Wow, I never thought of that." And the plan was formulated so that the smaller guest room would hold the bed, dresser, a comfortable chair, the TV, a small bookcase for DVDs and VHS tapes, and a piece of exercise equipment to be named later. The bottom drawer of the dresser would hold the guest linens. Susan would put her exercise clothes in the middle drawer. The top drawer would remain empty for guests to use.

The new, larger office would be big enough for the computer, most of the books, and the file cabinet. "All of my paperwork and files," declared Susan. And the rolltop desk.

"And since you're not very good with plants, I notice, how about some fish? Would you like some in your office or maybe the living room?"

"Oh, in my office, I think. How did you know I'd like an aquarium? I feel like you've known me forever!" Susan gushed. *A keen eye and a quick mind*, thought Pat.

***

By four o'clock there was a plan for the entire house, approved by Susan and endorsed by Pat, who proclaimed, "Excellent! We just have a couple more details to go over before we can call it a day."

"Okay, but before we do that, I want to call that sister of mine and let her know that she'll need to stop by in three weeks to check out my newly organized house. You see, the deal is that it has to meet her approval – which I'm sure it will – and it has to stay that way for six months. I'll put her on the speaker phone so you can hear."

"I really don't think that's necessary. You can call her …" Br-ring! Br-ring! "… after I leave." Pat protested quickly, but it was already too late.

"Dr. Huffman's office." The male voice sounded confident, but very laid back.

"Hi, Jon. It's Susan. Is my sister available?"

"Sure. I'll put you right through."

The call was put on hold and New Age music came over the speaker. "Honestly, Susan," protested Pat, "I don't like eavesdropping."

"Nonsense!" Susan's personality really did change to belligerent whenever Dr. Hellen was involved. "I want you to hear with your own ears that I didn't make up this payment story. I don't want you to have any doubt that there is a pot of gold at the end of this rainbow."

"What is it? I'm with a patient, you know," snapped, Pat assumed, Dr. Hellen.

"I'm sorry. Really. I didn't know. Jon just put me through, you see. No indication."

"Ha!" Dr. Hellen indicated disbelief. "Well, now that I've been interrupted, what is it?"

"I'm taking my three weeks of vacation and getting organized, you see. So I wanted you to come over two weeks from this Friday to have a look?"

"Why would I want to do that?"

"Didn't you say if I got the house organized and kept it that way for six months you'd pay me a hundred thousand dollars?"

"Ha! Yes, I said that. Like it'll ever happen!"

Pat wondered if Dr. Hellen's patient was in the room listening to this derision.

"Okay, I'll be there at two o'clock. It'll be worth the laugh. Ha!" Dr. Hellen clicked off without any other indication that the conversation was over.

"AAARGH! I'll show her!" shouted Susan.

Pat, who felt the same way as Susan, tried to sound nonplussed. "Yes, you will," she responded in a very quiet voice.

The whole Dr. Hellen incident made it difficult to complete the business of the day. But by five o'clock, the details were finalized. For the next three weeks, Susan would have nightly mini-assignments, but otherwise should do whatever she wanted in the evenings, so long as it didn't add to the disorganization. Pat would take Wednesdays for her other work, and Susan would be given larger tasks to accomplish on her own on Wednesdays. Susan would lose her bunny slippers in favor of sensible shoes, and Pat would lose her suit in favor of jeans and a sweatshirt.

"Susan, I think you've probably realized from the plan that you'll be deciding to get rid of a lot of stuff."

"Oh, yes, you see, I figure I'll probably get rid of about half of this clutter."

Oh, I would think more like three quarters of it. But Pat kept that thought to herself. "Well, not all of it is trash. You have a lot of usable things that you'll want to pass on to someone else who needs them. So, your assignment for tonight is to decide on two – no more, no less – two charities to donate to. You want to pick one that takes fairly worn and lower-valued items and one that takes the higher-end items. The great thing about donating is that you can take a tax deduction. I have a computer program I'll bring tomorrow that will let us catalog everything as we go and will calculate the highest tax value the IRS will accept."

"I'm so glad you didn't say 'yard sale.'"

"It's too late in the day to get me started on the downside of those!" laughed Pat. "Maybe some other time. I'll see you tomorrow at nine, with your shoes and your charities."

Chapter 6

Pat backed out of Susan's driveway and started toward home. In front of the bird feeder's house she pulled her car over to the curb and tapped on the hazard blinkers and the dome light. She needed to capture those three ideas she had come up with during the day for inclusion in one of her books. Pat had been collecting these thoughts for a number of months now. She didn't feel it was right to stop while she was with a client to make notes for her book, although if she were taking notes anyway she would scribble her idea in the margin. So, she at least tried to keep count in her head so she'd know how many ideas to recall at the end of the day. Today, there were three more after the first one she had written down about juniper bushes before she had even gotten out of her car this morning.

Pat pulled out an index card and wrote: Make a list of the types of light bulbs you need and keep one supply of them in one place in your house. She read the card and edited it on the spot by adding "(and batteries)" after the words "light bulbs" and by underlining, for emphasis, both occurrences of the word "one." Then she tossed the card into her briefcase and pulled out another one.

She wrote: Think of t-shirts (clothes) crammed in drawers as trapped little creatures begging for their freedom. Pat wasn't so sure if this one would work. Maybe she'd try it on Susan. And she wasn't sure if it would make it into her book. But it was good to capture the thought. She tossed this card in with the first one and pulled out one more.

She thought. And thought. Oh, crud! What was the third idea? It was probably the best one of the day. What was it? Think, think, think. WHAT WAS IT? Gone. Oh, well … Pat shut off the extra car lights and headed for home.

Fifteen minutes later, Pat unlocked her front door, turned on the light, and looked around. She saw the collection of shoes sitting just inside the door, the wilted plant in the corner, and the half-empty teacup and plate of cookie crumbs on the dining room table. In her mind, she saw her kitchen with the eggshells in the sink and the jumble of recipes on the counter. And Pat thought, as she often did upon returning from a client: my house really isn't so bad.

Pat changed into comfortable clothes and, forty-five minutes later, the chicken was seasoned and in the oven, the rice and asparagus were simmering on the stove, everything else was on the table, and Pat was going through the day's mail. There was a plate of cheese and crackers, along with a bottle of Chardonnay and two glasses waiting on the coffee table. Fred arrived and said, "Hi, Pat. Sure smells good." Then he planted an enthusiastic kiss on Pat's lips, poured them each a glass of wine, and declared, "To the love of my life!"

Pat smiled as she took a sip.

Chapter 7

Tuesday morning it was back to Susan's. Pat was already feeling a sense of attachment. The discarded Christmas tree had blown two houses away from its original home, but was securely braced against the tree on its new tree lawn. The city workers would collect it from here without ever knowing it had moved. The man was out filling his bird feeders again. He was a man with routines, and Pat chose to imagine that his house and life were in perfect order.

There was no fancy car parked at Susan's neighbor's. Susan's yard was still unkempt. Pat, the most successful organizer in the State, felt needed.

Kkrriiiiing! The door almost flew open! "Good morning!" sang Susan. "I am ready!" Pat was so taken aback that she stole a quick glance at Susan's feet before responding. But, sure enough, Susan had on good, solid athletic shoes. "Great!" returned Pat, hoping that the slight pause didn't make her enthusiasm sound fake. "So am I."

"Great! … Yeah, great," Susan's attitude seemed to be on an immediate wane. "Great," her voice was softer now, "but, you see, I still don't know where to start."

Pat didn't even have to think to respond. "That IS great. Because I have a plan in mind and I was hoping that I wouldn't have to convince you. But, since between us we only have one plan, then we're good to go.

"Were you a good girl? Did you do your homework and pick your two charities?"

"Oh, yes. You see, Upward House will take the really nice stuff and sell it to support their work. And St. Smith's will take anything else that's usable to give to poor families and victims of disasters. I picked them because they both do good work. And I think they'll both come get the stuff instead of me having to take it to them."

"Good choices. Here, let me show you how this donation software works. For each item, you have a choice of whether it's in excellent, very good, or good condition. Then it assigns the value listed in that column. The software automatically tabulates the items as you go. See, for example, that pasta maker you've never used would have a donated value of thirty dollars."

"That seems kind of high to me. I don't want to get into trouble with the Internal Revenue Service."

"The makers of the software guarantee the values."

"I don't know. It still seems high."

"You think a lot like I do. But, honest, my husband has an old college buddy who's now an attorney in the tax division of the Justice Department. He uses it himself and swears the government won't question it."

"I'm still dubious."

"Well, why don't we use the program anyway? If, in the end, you think the total seems unreasonably high, then you can always claim less on your tax return. That seems sensible, doesn't it?"

"Yeah, that's a pretty good idea. And, in any event,

I'll have what I really need, which is an itemized list of the contributions."

"Right." Pat hoped every little thing all day wasn't going to involve this much explanation and convincing. What they needed to do was build some speed and momentum if they were going to get through everything before Dr. Hellen arrived for her inspection in eighteen days, only eleven of which Pat would be on premises. "Now, let's get started. With the top shelf of the kitchen cabinets. I believe that will involve four sets of dishes."

"Yes, my grandmother's china, my mother's china, my college dishes, and the set with the odd-sized cups," Susan ticked them off as if she was sure that Pat would not have remembered.

"That's what I remembered," Pat affirmed, but in a tone that was upbeat rather than belying her annoyance. "Now, for a single woman such as yourself, I would suggest that one set of fine china and one set of everyday dishes would be appropriate."

"So …" Susan showed reluctance.

"So, start by telling me which of the two sets of good china you like better. And why."

"Well, you see, I positively adore my grandmother's set. The dainty little pansies remind me of her garden in the summer. And we used to have the best food off of those dishes. Just looking at them makes me happy inside."

"Then that's the set you should keep. Do you want to donate your mother's set to Upward House?"

"Oh, no! They were my mother's! And I had to fight to get them. Hellen thought they should be hers because she's older. But I traded her because she wanted Mother's mink stole, which Mother always said she wanted me to have. But I didn't want it. I don't like wearing dead animals. So, I told Hellen she could have it but only if she gave me the china. She protested and protested. But I pointed out that the mink was rightfully mine and worth way more than the china. So, in the end, she gave in. But she still mutters about me getting the china."

"Do you have another sister who might want it?"

"No, you see, there's just me, Hellen, and my brother Joe."

"How about Joe?"

"No, I don't think he'd want it. I wouldn't even want to ask him because I wouldn't want him to feel he had to take it out of obligation," Susan reasoned. Pat was considering whether to suggest that Joe should be able to make his own decisions when, all of a sudden, Susan got an expression on her face as if a diabolical light bulb had gone off. "Why don't I give them to Hellen? You see, that would show her that I'm really getting rid of stuff. And it would show her that I've risen above these petty arguments we're always having."

Pat kept her mouth shut, even though she thought there was compelling evidence that Susan was anything but over the being petty stage.

"And, you see, that way I'll keep the china in the family, too. Because I just can't give away an heirloom like that, can I?"

Pat resorted to a statement of general principle. "Well, you really shouldn't give away or sell a family heirloom until it's been offered to everyone in the family."

Pat and Susan moved Mother's china set to the living room where Susan would box it and send it to Hellen with a note of reconciliation that, mercifully, Pat would never have to see.

And so they moved on to the everyday dishes. Pat

had little trouble convincing Susan that a disadvantaged family would be grateful for the set with the odd-sized cups, and Susan readily admitted that there was virtually no chance that she would ever use those dishes again. "The color is so dated. And I hate washing the cups by hand." Susan moved the set into the garage, on the side designated for St. Smith's.

The college dishes were another matter. Susan agreed that she preferred her current well-maintained set of off-white dishes with pale pink trim to the chipped set of avocado ironstone. "But they hold so many good memories," she protested. "They remind me of the happiest times in college. My friends Katie and Barb and I had so many important conversations while eating off those plates."

"Do you have any photos of the three of you eating from them?" Pat opened the negotiation.

"I don't think so. If I do, they'd be up in the storage room. But I don't recall any such photo."

"Do Katie and Barb live nearby?"

"What?"

"When was the last time you got together with

Katie and Barb? Do they live nearby?"

"Katie lives just south of here, about ten miles away. Barb lives across the country."

"Do you ever see Katie?"

"No, I send her a card at Christmas. I haven't talked to her in about five years."

"Okay, then. What about this idea? Call up Katie and invite her over for lunch, tea, dinner, whatever you like. Serve her on the college plates. Remember the old days. Take a photo of the two of you. Keep a copy for each of you and send one to Barb. Maybe even call Barb while you're eating and include her in the conversation. Use your speakerphone. All three of you say a proper goodbye to the dishes with a commitment never to forget the memories. Then send the dishes on to a new home. What do you think?"

"It's a good idea." Susan hesitated. "But when will I find the time?"

"No time like the present. Call Katie right now. Invite her for lunch next Wednesday. I'll make it part of your Wednesday assignment."

"But," Susan continued to protest, "the house will be a mess."

"So what? Katie is an old friend, she knows you're cleaning things out, and won't it be all the more authentic? Surely you weren't neat when you were a student, were you?"

"Gosh, I feel like you've known me for years! You're right. I'll do it." So the calls were made, one assuring Katie's attendance (she was quite delighted!) and one encouraging Barb's telephonic participation (she didn't need much urging). Pat loaded the dishes into the dishwasher. Once clean, they would wait in the dining room for their big farewell party.

Pretty soon, *thank goodness*, Susan and Pat were humming along. At first Susan had seemed too distractible for the task – Pat would be asking her about one item and Susan would be focusing on another. So, Pat had Susan get her laptop and sit down with it at the kitchen table. Pat would hold up an item and ask, "Do you use it?"

If Susan's answer was "yes" then Pat placed the item on the kitchen counter. If Susan's answer was "no" then there were three alternatives: the trash, St. Smith's, or Upward House. Susan quickly dubbed this the "Use It or Lose It" method, and Pat made a mental note for a future index card. *Clients can be so clever and creative.*

At first, deciding where to send something and how to value it made it seem like the kitchen would take forever. Susan sighed, "You see, we'll never get through the whole house in three weeks."

"Well," Pat shifted into her genius gear, "the more detailed the plan the faster things tend to go. Why don't we establish some rules so we don't have to think so much about each item?" Susan squinted. Pat continued, "We're already using the rule that we're keeping what you use. For the stuff we're getting rid of, let's say that if it's broken or dirty, it goes in the trash. If it's never been used or it's from the baking club it goes to Upward House. And everything else goes to St. Smith's."

"Okay."

"And let's take it one step further. If it's going to Upward House, you key it in as having the highest value in that software. And if it's going to St. Smith's, you key it in with the lowest value. We'll ignore the middle value, and it should all average out."

"Okay!"

And that way, Pat and Susan got up to speed. Pat

held up an item and Susan called out the answer and keyed in the donations.

"St. Smith's. I used it for a couple of weeks." The juicer.

"Upward House. Never touched it." The waffle iron.

"Use it." Espresso maker.

"One for me, one to St. Smith's." The two pie pans.

Every time they finished a cabinet or drawer, Pat would take the St. Smith's items and Susan would take the Upward House items and carry them to their assigned sides of the garage. Every time a trash bag was filled, it went to the living room.

"Upward House." The springform pan.

"Upwar … no! wait! Do I have to follow the rule? I've never used it, but, you see, I want to." The electric hibachi.

"It's okay. We don't need to be draconian! You're doing really well here. You can keep the hibachi and see how it works out."

"Use it!" Pans one, two, three, four, and five in the set.

"Upward." Pans six, seven, eight, and nine.

"Smith's." An old frying pan that had been buried

in the back of the cabinet.

Another trip to the garage.

"Wait a second. I have no idea how many of those I use." Pat had held up the first of a cabinetful of plastic food storage containers.

Pat went on autopilot, launching into her standard plastic food storage container litany, reminding herself that while she found it boring and obvious, this was all new and enlightening to Susan.

"Do you have leftovers often? Do you usually use them before they start growing and looking like science projects? You really shouldn't keep anything in the first place if you know you won't eat it again. But anything you're not sure about should go in a food storage bag, so if it does get disgusting you can just pitch it and not have to deal with it or cleaning the container. Of course, liquids need the more rigid container instead of a plastic bag. And some things do better in plastic bags because you can squeeze out all the extra air. And there are the environmental considerations. And consider whether you cook ahead and freeze things.

"As general rules, you really don't want to keep any container that doesn't have a lid, or any lid that doesn't have a container. You could probably use four of each of the smaller sizes and two each of the larger sizes unless you have some special needs that you should tell me about." Pat peered into the cabinet. "Now, the first thing you should tell me is which style you prefer, these ones with the blue lids or the ones with the white lids. Consider which ones are easier to scrape things out of, whether one set stacks better than the other, if one set tends to stain, which ones are easier to clean, if some of them work better in the freezer. What do you think?"

"I think …" Susan furrowed her brow. "Hmm. I think that the ones with the blue lids are better in the freezer, but the ones with the white lids are easier to close."

The unmatched tops and bottoms went in the trash. Susan kept two of each size of both the blue-lidded and white-lidded types. The rest went to St. Smith's.

That took them to the last cabinet, the one with all the cookbooks. "I used to belong to the cookbook-of-the-month club," Susan explained sheepishly. She knew she wanted to keep her two favorite cookbooks "which I really use" and her mother's cookbook "because it makes me feel happy even if I don't use it. I guess you could say I don't use it for the recipes but I do use it to make me feel good." She was trying so hard to follow the rules.

The other cookbooks were more problematic. The first one was a book of pies and Susan thought she might need a good peach pie recipe someday. She responded to the second book with, "What if I decide I want to cook a Greek dinner sometime?" *Patience, Patience.* Pat patiently had Susan open her web browser and search for "peach pie recipe." 10,400 hits. Then "Greek recipe." 7,920,000.

"I don't need any of these other cookbooks," Susan announced. Pat started to move the books to the garage, but she thought that this was even an easier sell than she could have hoped.

Here it was, lunchtime, and they had been through everything in the kitchen. Susan was shocked that everything she had decided to keep fit on the tops of her counters; it just didn't seem like much at all. "Once we put this stuff back in the cabinets and drawers, what will I do with the empty ones?"

"Well, first we'll have to see how much extra space you'll really have. And before we do that, we'll have to attack that wall of food you have in your basement." There, Pat had, without letting on that she felt guilty, admitted that she had dubbed Susan's stash the Wall of Food. "That's where we'll start after lunch."

Susan followed Pat to the door, and Pat left her with the standard lunchtime admonishment, "Don't forget to eat something to keep your energy up."

***

When Susan opened the door after Pat's pb&j sandwich lunch break – after all, it had not been a very trying morning – Pat thought that Susan looked a little concerned. And she was right.

Rather than engaging in the usual, somewhat meaningless, social pleasantries, Susan blurted, "I have a confession to make, you see. While you were gone, I went out to the garage ..."

Uh-oh, I wonder how much stuff got moved back into the kitchen? But, it turned out not to be bad at all.

"... and I dug out my old cookbook from college. You see, I think I'll cook some of our old favorites for next Wednesday. And I think I'd like to keep the book, too." Susan stopped and looked at Pat as if waiting for her punishment.

"Makes sense to me," affirmed Pat, with an internal sigh of relief. She followed Susan into the kitchen where tea was waiting.

Pat decided to tackle the subject of Susan and Pat's relationship. "You know, Susan," she began tentatively. But Pat didn't ever do much tentatively, and almost immediately launched forward full steam and with confidence, "I don't want you to view me as your adversary, as someone you have to be on the defensive with who will always push against you. I'm here to help you make the decisions you want to make. I'll never make you throw out something you want to keep. I'll just ask you to make sure that you really want to keep it. In fact," and here Pat knew as soon as she started that she was overstating how she felt, "if you don't succeed in satisfying your sister and she doesn't give you the money, but you're happy, I'll still be glad I helped you." *Gosh, I hope I don't have to eat those words.*

"Oh, Pat!," Susan rushed around the table and gave Pat a big hug. "I know I picked the right organizer. Thank goodness! Thank you!" Then she added in a totally unflattering and belligerent voice, "But that sister of mine better pay up!"

Mental note: Try not to mention Dr. Hellen. "You know, I never did ask you how you found me." Pat was truly curious and this gave her the opportunity to sway the conversation back toward the more factual, rather than emotional, side.

"Well, you see, I looked on the Internet and I found three professional organizers that lived around here. I called the first one – it wasn't you – and got an answering machine. She sounded so hurried, like she was trying to cram a sixty-second commercial into ten seconds. And the message said 'I' this and 'me' that. Kind of sounded like that louse of a sister I have, and I didn't think I could handle that. So I just hung up without leaving a message. Then I called you – I almost didn't because I was beginning to think the idea of getting a professional organizer was not going to work, but I dialed your number and you answered right away. And you seemed so genuinely concerned – and I couldn't bear the thought of making another call and maybe getting someone like the first organizer – so I just decided to try you. And I'm so glad I did!" she added.

Just another key to being the most successful organizer in the State. "And I'm glad you did, too."

Over tea, they mapped out where things would go in the kitchen – heavier things in the lower cabinets so they wouldn't fall out and damage something or someone, most-used items within easy reach, seasonal items tucked away a bit.

Then it was downstairs to the Wall of Food, where they created a new set of rules. Anything that was out of date by more than six months would be trashed. Everything else would either be kept IN THE KITCHEN if Susan thought she would use it or given to the food bank at the church down the road.

As the afternoon and their energy wound down, Pat and Susan surveyed their accomplishments. The kitchen was totally purged and organized, and the Wall of Food was gone.

Pat sat down at the kitchen table and, pulling out a piece of paper, asked, "What day is your trash pickup?"

"Monday."

"What time on Monday?"

"Usually mid-afternoon."

"Perfect!" Pat could hardly believe it would work out so well.

"Why do you say that?" Susan was curious.

"You'll see." *Oh no, I hope I'm not starting to sound like my client. I hate it when I do that.* "So, let me write down your assignments for tomorrow. They'll be:

"Get boxes for the stuff for St. Smith's and Upward House.

"Phone St. Smith's and arrange pickup on third Wednesday.

"Phone Upward House and arrange pickup on third Wednesday.

"Phone and schedule movers for two weeks from Thursday, in the morning.

"Send china set to Hellen.

"Take food to the church food bank."

Pat looked up at Susan. "Okay, then, you know which movers to call, right?"

"Yep."

"And we're agreed that you'll leave the trash bags in the living room until Monday, right?'

"Yep."

"Okay, then there's just one more thing I want to

add to your list." Pat opened up her case and pulled out a tiny brown paper bag, the kind they put screws and other little things in when you buy them at the hardware store. This bag was the very thing that Pat had procured from the hardware store in the shopping center where she had lunch on Monday. She handed it to Susan and wrote on the list, "Fill little paper bag with old cosmetics to throw out."

"What's this for?" asked Susan as Pat wrote.

"Well, we haven't talked about cleaning out your bathroom, but I did notice that you have a lot of cosmetics sitting out. I want you to fill this bag with three or four of the ones that need to be thrown out. I know to do it all is a big job, but just having to fill this little bag will keep it manageable for you to start on your own."

"But there's nothing to throw out," came the protest. "Those all cost a lot of money and none of them are used up."

"Yes, but you can't possibly use them all before they become dangerous. Cosmetics that touch you directly – anything with brushes, sponges, or other applicators – only have a usable life of six months. And you can't give them away, because it's a health risk." Pat confidently stated these facts while knowing full well that she did not follow these guidelines with her own cosmetics. Those little bottles of makeup lasted an incredibly long time at the rate Pat used them. Then again, Pat didn't have more than a half dozen bottles, while Susan had about a hundred.

"That can't be." It was getting late and Susan was tired and becoming defiant.

"Well, let's look it up." Pat pulled over the laptop. In less than a minute she had an article explaining the hazards of germs breeding in cosmetics more than six months old.

"Wow, I never knew that," acquiesced Susan. "Okay, I guess I can fill up this tiny bag."

"That's the spirit!" *Mental note: third-party authorities in writing, even from the Internet, carry great weight and can serve as motivators.*

"Great," continued Pat. "Then that wraps it up for today. You have your work for tomorrow, and I'll see you again Thursday morning."

"Thanks, again." Susan opened the door for Pat, gave her another hug, and sent her out into the crisp, early evening air.

Pat made a very quick stop down the street, just to make index cards about "use it or lose it" and the power of the Internet.

As she drove toward home she felt great, with a sense of true satisfaction. She had learned a couple of things herself, and she had taught a good deal to Susan and left her in a good mood. This job might just pay off after all. And, on top of that, tomorrow was her day off.

Chapter 8

"Day off! What a misnomer. At best, it's a change of pace day." Pat was muttering to herself as she was drinking her second cup of very strong coffee – coffee being reserved for days when it was particularly hard, yet important, to get going.

Pat's original plan when she had signed on with Susan Huffman was to have Wednesdays to herself to write her book. But almost as soon as she had formulated that plan, she had accepted a lunchtime speaking engagement for this very Wednesday. It was a basic enough talk to give, time management for stay-at-home parents. She had presented it many times. Yet, here she was, the morning of the talk, having to scramble around to create the custom cover for the handouts – the most successful organizer in the State always created a custom cover – make the copies, and come up with some tailored opening and closing sentences to make it sound like today's audience was her one and only purpose in life – tailored comments being another key to her status as the most successful organizer in the State.

Pat loved public speaking. Truth be told, after eight years of organizing in the trenches, nothing would make her happier than if she could give presentations and write for a living. She believed that getting her first book published would be the breakthrough point in achieving this dream. But, for some reason, she still had not written the book.

And here was another day she should have firmly set aside, yet she had not. She could dish out the advice to her clients and expect them to follow it, but she had trouble with it herself. Hypocritical? Perhaps. Or perhaps it was what made her so in tune with her clients and their plights.

But, as much as she liked an audience, Pat really didn't care much for these lunchtime talks. They were better than breakfast talks, which required her to get up in the wee hours in order to be alert when she took the stage, but that was about it.

What didn't she like about them? For one thing, there was the compensation structure. Unlike workshops, breakout conference sessions, keynotes, and seminars, the pay for mealtime talks was basically nonexistent. If she pressed, she could sometimes extract a two-figure honorarium, a mere fraction of her usual speaking fee. Lately, she had decided it wasn't worth the effort and discomfort of the discussion; she would simply state that she would give the presentation without fee but would be happy to accept any honorarium the group might choose to give her. She came out about the same financially – sometimes better – without the hassle.

What groups did like to offer was free food. And Pat loved to eat. She loved to sample food from places she didn't usually go. But there was a problem here, too. The meals were always served immediately before the program. And Pat found that if she filled her stomach before getting up to speak, not only would her audience be fighting off the post-meal drowsies, but she would be, as well. Then she would give a rather mediocre presentation with which she was not at all satisfied.

Once, early on in her career, she had been hired – actually for pay! – to speak at a luncheon workshop at a major company. She had been told by the event coordinator that the employees would bring brown bag lunches. Pat had, wisely she thought, decided she would eat after her presentation. But, when she arrived, it turned out the coordinator had decided to have lunch catered – and the menu was Mexican food. Pungent Mexican food. Pat began to salivate like Pavlov's dogs and her stomach would not stop rumbling. "Smells good," Pat had commented flatly to her host. "Feel free to have some," had come the reply. But Pat was scheduled to talk throughout the lunch hour and she couldn't figure out how she was supposed to eat a taco and present a seminar at the same time. As the employees attacked their food with gusto, and Pat's stomach continued to rumble, Pat had presented her material. Afterward, the coordinator said that she had found the presentation to be somewhat lackluster. Pat doubted that the well-fed attendees had noticed. Still, the memory haunted her as one of the worst of her career.

Pat came to the realization that, while her

lunchtime talks were always billed as educational, what luncheon guests were really looking for was entertainment. So, being the most successful organizer in the State, Pat had developed a formula of edutainment for such events, with the goals of leaving the audience happy and, possibly, inclined to send some paying business Pat's way.

***

Pat checked her computer-generated map directions – maybe she should consider getting GPS – and turned into the private driveway. As she approached the gatehouse, her morning disgruntlement began melting away. She remembered that the good part of these luncheon talks was that she got to go places that would otherwise have been closed to her.

As she pulled to a stop, the guard came out of his shelter, clipboard in hand, and gave her an inquiring look. What a double personality job he must have, thought Pat. He needs to greet everyone pleasantly on the assumption that they really do qualify for admittance. But he would have to turn quickly to a no-nonsense enforcer if he needed to turn someone away.

Pat rolled down her window and offered her

business card. "I'm Patience Oaktree, the speaker at today's women's luncheon."

The guard checked his clipboard, looked at her card, and then walked in front of her minivan to copy down her license plate number. He returned to the window and handed her a laminated placard. "Here you go, Ms. Oaktree. Just place that on your dashboard and then return it here when you leave."

"Thanks, Mr. Kowalsky." Pat hoped she had not squinted too noticeably as she read the guard's name badge. She was a firm believer that addressing people by name made them feel more important and more inclined to be helpful. Such a small thing to do for such significant rewards. "Could you tell me, please, where the most convenient place for me to park would be?"

"Take the first left and then get as close to the building as you can. The door is on the right, so try to park on that side even if you have to walk a little farther. That way you'll avoid having to climb over any snow drifts."

"Okay, thanks." Pat rolled up the window and headed toward the building. *Kowalsky, Kowalsky, Kowalsky*, she repeated to herself until she had pulled into a parking space. Then she took out a sticky note, wrote the name on it, and stuck it on the inside of the car door. There was no other way she knew to be sure she would remember the guard's name two hours from now.

Pat pulled open the massive wood door, and stepped inside the clubhouse. An absorbent rug had been placed inside, so that by the time Pat had crossed to the short marble staircase leading up to the main area, the bottoms of her shoes were dry. The ceiling in the reception hall was at least twenty feet high, with three large brass chandeliers. A shiny black grand piano, just far enough from the crackling fireplace so that the heat wouldn't cause it to go out of tune, was being played by a young man dressed in formal attire. Pat noticed that this place was very, as she would term it, Emily Post – the pianist was not wearing a tuxedo, which would of course be inappropriate at this time of day; no, he was wearing a proper morning coat. He was playing Chopin études, some of Pat's favorites.

Pat stood behind two other women at the luncheon registration table. Then she introduced herself to the woman taking names. "Hi, Becky." –

another nametag had clued her in – "I'm Pat Oaktree, today's speaker. We spoke on the phone; it's nice to meet you in person."

"Oh, it's sooo nice to meet you. We're so glad you could join us." The two shook hands. "Here's your nametag. You'll want to wear it after you take off your coat." Becky gestured toward the coat room, which, Pat was happy to see, appeared to be self-serve. "We have mix-and-mingle time for a half hour before lunch, so make yourself at home."

Pat hung up her coat, straightened her hair, slipped the official nametag into her pocket in case it would be required to be served lunch, and clipped on her own nametag which included the emblems of her professional associations. Then she set about the pre-event working of the crowd.

She approached two women standing near the brass and mahogany bar who didn't seem to be involved in too heavy a conversation. When they paused, she began, "Hello. I didn't want to interrupt you, but I did want to introduce myself. I'm Pat Oaktree, your …"

"Our speaker!" gushed the taller of the women, who was dressed in a very fashionable suit that Pat would classify as more social than business attire. "We are so excited to have you here! I'm Marcia Sturdy." And, indeed, that's what the felt-tipped marker letters on her adhesive-backed nametag, plastered on her thousand-dollar suit, said.

Oh my goodness, thought Pat. This woman is married to Patrick Sturdy, the highest-paid corporate executive in the City. Maybe, if I'm lucky, she'll mention me to her husband.

Before Pat could say anything more, the other woman, who was demurely stirring a martini with a plastic sword toothpick full of green olives, chimed in, "Oh, yes! We were both just saying how much we're looking forward to your ideas on how to clean out our garages."

Pat was about to try to diplomatically tell them that her topic of the day was time management, when Gretchen, the woman with the martini, caught the arm of another woman heading toward the bar. "Mary, let me introduce you to our speaker, Pat Oaktree."

"Pat. Nice to meet you. Can I get you a drink?"

Pat looked at Marcia's Bloody Mary, and Gretchen's martini, and thought how lovely it would be to say yes and to spend the lunch hour as a lady of the Club. "No, thanks. That's very nice, but I do have a presentation to give," she smiled.

"Are you sure?" Mary pressed, making it harder for Pat to keep her resolve.

"Yes, I'm sure," Pat answered regretfully.

"Okay, then," Mary sang as she moved closer to the bar. "You know, I was going to clean out my closet yesterday, but then I thought I'd wait until tomorrow after I learned all your wonderful tips."

By the time mix-and-mingle was over, Pat had talked to quite a few of local society's most prominent women. She had managed to suppress the thought that these women could easily have paid her full speaker's fee; it would have been less than the cost of one pair of their shoes. She had also learned that they wanted to know how to organize garages, closets, children's toys, and butler's pantries. It seemed none of them felt challenged in the time management department.

Becky steered Pat to her table for lunch. The conversation turned toward the local school levy, and Pat was content not to have to talk about organizing for a few minutes. She sipped on her caffeine-laden iced tea, while the other ladies enjoyed a Sauvignon Blanc, and she just picked at her tossed salad, which was nothing special.

The entrée was another matter. A wonderful nut-encrusted pan-fried walleye with asparagus spears and a sumptuous lemon and wine reduction sauce. Pat savored the five bites she allowed herself.

"Are you finished?" asked the waiter when he came to take the plates.

Pat was still hungry and looked longingly at the expertly prepared meal that she had barely touched. She ventured, "Could you wrap up what's left so I can take it home?"

"I beg your pardon?"

"I'm the guest speaker and I need to make my presentation now. But I would hate to waste such a wonderful meal; it's absolutely delicious," Pat tried to win the waiter to her side. She wished she knew his name. "I would really enjoy being able to have it later."

"Well, we usually don't do that sort of thing. I'll have to see if we have anything to put it in," huffed the waiter.

"Well, I don't mean to cause any trouble or

inconvenience," whispered Pat who was a bit worried that her hosts would find this whole exchange to be rather rude. "You can just take it away, then." She tried to put just enough wistfulness in her voice to make the waiter feel guilty. He picked up the plate.

Becky rose to introduce Pat, and Pat turned to the person next to her and asked her to please make sure they saved Pat's dessert for her to enjoy after the presentation. Gosh, she hoped it wouldn't be, as it so many times was, ice cream.

Pat began passing around her handouts. She heard Becky reading her prepared bio, the last line of which would be her cue, the line that said, "Pat's topic today is the Key Elements of Household Time Management." Instead she heard Becky say, "And now here's Pat to teach us all how to get organized."

Pat sprinted to the front of the room, smiling, with her mouth on autopilot doing the usual thank-you-for-having-me-I'm-so-happy-to-be-here spiel, while her mind raced. She was prepared to speak on time management, her handout made that clear, but this group wanted to hear about garages and closets. Well, never mind, Pat could handle this.

So Pat told the group that in light of what she had learned from her lovely talks with them all before lunch, she had decided to condense her prepared remarks which they could read more about on their own in the written materials. Then she opened the floor up to questions for the remaining forty-five minutes.

"How do I keep my son's basketballs from rolling under the wheels of the car when I drive into the garage?"

"Have you tried a garbage can to hold them? Or, if it's only one or two balls there's a great claw-type thing you can hang on the wall. You shove the ball into it and it holds it in place until you pull the ball back out .... Yes, I can send you the information on it if you write down your email address for me."

"How can I hang my six-year-old's dresses where she can reach them?"

"I guess the standard solution is mounting a lower bar in the closet. But, if you want something more temporary and stylish, you can use the dowels on a blanket rack. They are the perfect height for a six-year-old and her clothes."

And on it went. At the end of the hour people

were rushing up to Pat with more questions and asking when she could come back. Pat returned to her seat where she was looking forward to enjoying the flourless chocolate torte – not melted ice cream! – that she had watched being served and eaten as she spoke. The torte was still at her place, but it was clear that everyone was leaving. On Pat's chair was a classy plastic bag with the Club's logo. At first she thought this might be a token gift from the women's group, but when she looked inside, she saw a plastic clamshell container with her leftover lunch. Pat stealthily slipped the torte in on top, said her thank-yous and goodbyes, and was out the door.

"Thank you, again, Mr. Kowalsky," she said as she turned in the guest parking pass. "Keep warm."

***

When she got home, Pat microwaved the lunch. She thought about making herself a Bloody Mary – the ones at the Club had looked so good – but she decided that drinking by herself in the middle of the day was not the thing to do. She was just sitting down when the phone rang. The caller-ID showed that it was Fred.

"Hi, Fred. I'm glad it's you."

"I thought you might be home by now. How was the ritzy lunch?"

"The presentation went great. Even though I had to speak on something altogether different than what I'd planned."

"I knew they'd love you. How was the food?"

"What I had of it was delicious. I'm just sitting down to the rest of it now. Although I guess it was a huge faux pas for me to ask for a doggie bag. I really don't get it – the waiter made it sound like it was never done, but in the end they had clamshell containers and everything. So, I don't know what the big deal was. But I hope I wasn't too gauche."

"I'm sure you weren't. I'll let you eat it before it gets cold again. Love you."

"Love you, too."

"Ppch."

Pat enjoyed every last bite.

Chapter 9

Thursday morning, of course, found Pat acknowledging her own mess, jiggling her door handle, and heading back to Susan Huffman's. As she drove past the modest homes on Susan's street, she thought about how far removed this all was from the opulence of yesterday's gig at the Club. Removed, and yet really the same. Those wealthy women were struggling with the same organizing situations as Susan, messy closets and garages. Pat half expected to see the Porsche again as a confirmation of the confluence of the wealthy and the middle class, but neither Mr. Rich Gorgeous nor his car was there.

Susan greeted Pat with a crisis. "Before we do anything, we need to talk. I've made us some tea." Susan headed toward the kitchen and Pat followed.

Pat had almost assumed that Susan would "hit the wall" during the second week, and she had been counting on the college reunion lunch to re-energize Susan. What could possibly have happened to cause this meltdown so soon? Maybe Pat had hurried Susan too much, and now she was having second thoughts about getting rid of so many of her possessions. Maybe Susan just needed a pep talk. Maybe ...

"Here, listen to this!" Susan tried to shout indignantly, but her voice caught as she forced back more tears. She clicked on the answering machine. Pat should have guessed – Susan's nemesis, the matchless Dr. Hellen!

The recording of Hellen's voice was short and blunt. And, yes, one could even say it cackled. "I can't believe you didn't want Mom's precious china! Oh well, I donated it to the hospital thrift shop." It was impossible to tell if Hellen's tone was serious or sarcastic.

Pat quickly ran through the series of options that

her response could take – indignant, dismissive, derogatory …. She settled on consoling. "Oh, Susan," she put her arm around Susan's shoulders, "don't take it so hard. You told me yourself that if Hellen didn't want it you would donate it to charity. Maybe your sister is just jealous that you're making real progress in improving your life."

"Maybe," sobbed Susan. She wrapped her hands around her teacup and stared into it. Pat wondered if she were looking for solace or her future.

After several minutes of sipping tea in silence, Pat announced, as though nothing unpleasant had occurred at all, "Well, today we're going to tackle your bedroom!" And Susan followed Pat up the stairs with no protest whatsoever.

The first order of business was to remove from the room all of the stuff that didn't belong – old mail, magazines, books – generally paperwork. They lugged all of it down to the spare bedroom that would become Susan's office.

"Shouldn't we be going through all this stuff instead of shuffling it around?" Susan wanted to know.

"No, I think if we get bogged down in the

paperwork we'll feel defeated. While it's generally a good idea not to shuffle stuff around, sometimes we have to move big chunks of things a few times before we get them into position for the real sorting work."

"Okay, then. To the office it goes!"

When they actually got to sorting out the clothes, Susan was amazed by some of the simple systems that Pat suggested.

Pat showed Susan how to fold her socks so she could place them in the drawer side by side instead of on top of each other. That way, Susan could see the entire assortment at once and remove whatever pair she selected without turning the remaining ones into a jumble.

They made room on the closet floor for the three laundry baskets and designated each one for a particular load of laundry – lights, darks, whites. Susan could toss and sort her dirty clothes at the same time. While Pat admitted she didn't understand why some people couldn't seem to take the extra step of opening the hamper lid to throw in the clothes, she did get rid of Susan's guilt by telling her that this was a more common happening than anyone would believe. The hamper was removed to the St. Smith's pile in the garage.

They made room in the drawers for all of Susan's clothes so that she wouldn't mind emptying the laundry baskets once the clothes were clean and folded. At first it had seemed impossible to Susan that she would want to part with any of her clothes. So Pat showed her how to start with the items in the bottom of the drawers first. Those things on the bottom, Pat explained, were the ones you wore least. Usually the bottom third of the contents of a drawer went untouched year after year. Anything out of style, pilled, frayed, or stained was dismissed. They did set aside one small drawer in the nightstand for "nostalgia" clothes – Susan's sorority sweater (which she admitted she wouldn't even wear to next Wednesday's lunch), a t-shirt with her name on it from her favorite theme park, a pair of pajamas her grandmother had sewn for her.

The only really emotional moment came when Susan found one sweater ravaged by moths. "Oh, no! You see, this is the sweater I knit at school when I didn't feel like studying. It took me hours and hours to knit this fancy pattern. And now it's full of holes!"

"Yes, but it did serve its purpose of letting you procrastinate on your studies," offered Pat. Pat had to admit it had been a truly gorgeous sweater. "Your knitting is beautiful," she continued. "Maybe you'll start to knit again after you're organized."

"Yes, I could do that," agreed Susan, "but I'll use acrylic yarn instead of wool! I don't want any more moths."

They had a moment of silence in memory of the formerly glorious sweater, wrapped it in an equally holey blanket as a sort of funeral shroud, and wished it well on its journey to the landfill.

Due respects having been paid to the dearly departed, they went back to work.

***

As the day wound to a close, Pat gave Susan her homework assignment. "Take forty-five minutes and throw out as many magazines as you can find that are more than two issues old."

"But, you see, I haven't read them yet," came back the standard objection that Pat knew so well.

"If the magazine really thrilled you, you would have read it as soon as it arrived." Pat's standard answer. "If you want to read the back issues you'll have to go to the library. Don't worry, they'll have them."

"Well, it'll be tough, but I'll try." Susan was unwilling to commit, although Pat could tell that she agreed with the reasoning.

"And tomorrow is supposed to be a little warmer, so I think we'll tackle the garage. Better wear an extra layer," Pat concluded. "Have a good evening."

"You, too."

Chapter 10

The garage clearing proved a little more problematic than Pat had anticipated. But, being hesitant not to take advantage of the break in the weather, she had been insistent that they continue. The difficulty was working around the growing mounds of boxes designated for St. Smith's and Upward House. And, of course, there was still the rolltop desk. But they had worked out a system to handle the clutter that lined the three walls, and now they were moving along at a pretty good clip.

It was shortly after lunch and Pat and Susan were still in the garage when they heard the distant kriiiing of the doorbell, a pounding on the front door, and a man's voice calling, "Hey, Sis, are you home?"

"Joe!" Susan dropped the bag of weed killer she was moving, creating a cloud of toxic dust. "It's my brother, Joe!" she called excitedly over her shoulder to Pat as she ran back into the house through the kitchen door. Pat carefully set down the bag of fertilizer she was handling and followed after Susan.

Joe was just barely able to put down the two large shopping bags he was carrying in time to catch Susan as she threw her arms around him. Clearly, Susan has a much different relationship with her brother than with her sister, thought Pat.

Joe returned the hug enthusiastically and then pushed Susan back to arm's length so he could study her. "You look happy! ... busy, but happy," he determined. "I stopped by the benk, but they said that you were on vacation. I'm glad I found you at home."

"You see, you're starting to sound like you're from oop noorth," Susan teased as she mimicked his accent.

"Huh?"

"It's a bank, not a benk."

But Joe had stopped listening as he looked past Susan and saw the living room full of garbage bags. "Yoo're not moving, are you?"

It was Susan's turn to say, "Huh?" Then, as she followed his gaze, "Oh, no! I've just accepted a challenge from Hellen to get the house organized. She promised me a hundred grand if I do it."

"What makes you think she'll pay oop?" The words flew out of Joe's mouth before he had thought. He quickly continued, so no answer was needed, "Speaking of Hel, look what I found." He motioned to the shopping bags. "I stopped by the hospital to see her on my way into town, but she was tied oop with patients. So I went doon to the Thrift Stoor, and they had this great set of china just like the one of Mother's that Hel always wanted. So, I bought it for her. Only thirty boocks. Do you think she'll like it?"

"As she would say, 'ha!'" came Susan's retort. "I doubt it. Seeing as that IS Mother's china. I gave it to Hellen, you see, because I was cleaning it out, and she always said she wanted it, and I wanted her to see that I really was making progress. But she just said 'ha!' the way she always does and criticized me for not wanting it. Then, she sent it off to the Thrift Store. I guess she only liked complaining about not having it." This all answered any doubt Pat had about whether Hellen Huffman had really given the china away.

"Well, now, that creates a dilemma. Should I give it to her as if I don't know, and see what she says? Should I tell her I'm insulted she didn't offer it to me if she didn't want it? Should I just hold it over her and tell her she wasn't fast enough getting to the Thrift Stoor and 'finders keepers'? ... I guess that's a trilemma, isn't it?" Joe chuckled.

Pat had a sense that she really liked Joe. She appreciated his lightheartedness and his wit, and Susan seemed truly happy in his presence. So, when Joe said, "Hey, Sis, aren't you going to offer me one of yoor famous pots of tea?" and Susan begged Pat to join them even though she and Susan had just finished tea forty-five minutes earlier, Pat was happy to accept. Especially when Joe bribed her by saying, "Then I'll help you guys finish oop in the garage, so you won't get behind."

Even better, Joe had brought authentic Scottish

shortbread – full of real, pure, delicious butterfat – to go with the tea. Pat happily munched and sipped as Susan and Joe caught up. Joe's contract installing new inventory software at a large corporation "oop noorth" was going very well and accounted for his new accent.

Before the teapot was empty, they also relived a few memories. "And remember the time Hel got mad at Dad for not letting her go to that sloomber party, and she refused to talk at the dinner table. Weren't those the best two weeks!"

Pat pondered about what type of personality would be able to keep its mouth shut for two whole weeks. And she mused about Joe's nickname for his older sister. Just as she was sure his use of "Sis" for Susan was not meant to imply she was a sissy, she was confident there was no perjorative behind the diminutive of Hellen's name that he used. No doubt, in his mind, it was a three-letter name. Still, Pat would bet that every time he said it, Susan visualized it with a double *l*. It brought back to mind that longstanding Shakespearean question, "What's in a name?" *Patience!*

Joe's added brawn and the spark he kindled in

Susan made the rest of the garage work go very well. Susan was particularly pleased that Joe said he would like to have the three brand-new bird feeders. "I always admire the man down the street, but, you see, I kept forgetting I'd already bought a feeder …. I think for now I'll leave the birds in that nice man's organized hands." Joe also said he could use Susan's extra spreader. Pat was starting to wonder if Joe didn't have a clutter problem himself. *Uh-uh-uh … don't be judgmental. Especially when you know you have two spreaders in your own garage.* Pat would have to remember to talk to Fred about that.

***

Pat left Susan and Joe trying to decide whether they wanted Japanese or Thai food for dinner. As she pulled out onto the street, she flipped open her cell phone and pressed speed dial number two for Fred.

After two rings, "This is Frederic Watson."

"This is Patience Oaktree," Pat mimicked back.

"Oh, hi," Pat could hear Fred's smile. "What's up?"

"I just left my client's. Say, I was wondering, do you think tomorrow we could go through some of those piles of tools in the basement?"

"Oh." Fred's voice was flat. Then, "You've just spent a whole week going through someone else's stuff. I think you deserve a break." Was Fred being conscientious or just coming up with a good excuse to procrastinate? Probably a little of both. "I was thinking we could go to that new art exhibit at the museum."

"You're right. That sounds like a good change of pace, and a lot more fun." Pat didn't need Fred to twist her arm. "That's what we'll do. For now, I'm headed home. I'll get the wine and appetizers ready."

"What kind of appetizers?"

"Oh, I thought I'd make a little paté out of the leftover trout and put it on water crackers with some olives on the side."

"Sounds delicious. I'll be home in about an hour."

"Great. I love you."

"I love you, too. Ppch."

Chapter 11

Week Two of the Susan Huffman project went along quite well.

Monday was a particularly bitter cold day, temperatures not expected to rise out of the teens. But at least there was no new snow to shovel before Pat left home. As she approached Susan's house, she noticed once again the black Porsche in the neighbor's driveway. Pat turned off her engine and carefully looked over the backside of the sports car. She marveled at how its owner could keep it so shiny with all of the salt spray from the winter roads. It seemed almost unreal, sort of like Rich

Gorgeous's hair. This time she also noticed the vanity license plate: LANDMAN. She wondered if that was Rich's last name. Or his profession. Or something to do with a hobby. She wanted to keep speculating, to be able to watch the car just a little longer in hopes that its owner would make an appearance. But, after five minutes, she realized that she would have to get about the work of the day without an uplifting glimpse of Mr. Gorgeous.

Pat and Susan spent a good bit of the morning dealing with the thirty-eight large bags of trash that had taken over all remaining space in Susan's living room.

First Pat asked, "So how do you feel about all this trash?"

"Sort of ashamed to be sending it all to the landfill." This was not the kind of response Pat had been expecting, but she went with it.

"Well, if you kept it, you would just have your own personal, unofficial landfill. And the stuff couldn't even decompose, because you can't live in a house full of compost. So, you're better off sending it to the designated landfill and letting the professionals deal with it. About all you can do is try not to be such a big contributor in the future. You know, the old 'reduce, reuse, recycle.' And I'd put the emphasis on reduce."

Pat went on, "But, here's what I really want you to tell me. Take a couple of minutes and focus on these bags. Think about what we put in them. Tell me if you can think of anything you regret throwing away. Anything you wish you were keeping."

"Hmm … no … no. No … um … no." Pat was glad Susan was taking the question seriously. "I don't think so. Let's see …." Pat was becoming hopeful there really would be nothing. "Well, maybe. Yeah, I guess the one thing that keeps coming back to mind is that old wooden picture frame with the cracked glass. Remember, we threw it out because the glass was broken and the wood was scratched and I didn't like the photo?"

"I do remember some deliberation about it." Pat's recollection actually was rather fuzzy. "So, do you want to keep it?"

"How can I?! It's buried in one of these bags."

"But will you wish you had it back once the trash collectors take it away?"

"I might. Yes, you see, I might."

"Then we'll have to dig it out." And with that pronouncement, Pat went to the garage and brought in a plastic garbage can. She lined it with a new trash bag, opened one of the filled bags in the living room, and began systematically moving the trash from the old bag to the new bag. When the first bag was finished, she sealed up the bag in the can, took it out, replaced it with the newly emptied bag, and moved on to the next filled bag. An hour and a half later, they found the picture frame in the nineteenth bag.

"That was a big waste of time!" declared Susan.

"Don't you want it after all?" asked Pat in her best nondisturbed voice.

Susan was clutching the frame, "Oh, yes! I'm very happy to have it! But it took a whole hour and a half. I guess I should have kept it in the first place."

"You can't beat yourself up about it," explained Pat. "We all make the wrong decisions sometimes – about throwing things out, or about acquiring them in the first place. But we do our best anyway. The important thing here is that you don't have any regrets about the rest of the stuff in these bags. We've just been back through nineteen of them, and you didn't want anything in them except the frame. My guess is you're feeling pretty confident about the other bags, as well. So, you shouldn't think of it as time wasted."

Susan did see some sense to that analysis, especially since she really did like the frame. They hauled the thirty-eight bags out to the curb. Pat took out a Polaroid camera and snapped two shots of Susan standing with one foot resting on the bags, looking like queen of the mountain. They hurried back inside from the cold.

When the photos developed, Pat captioned them "good riddance!" and had Susan sign them. She explained to Susan that it was important for Susan to feel triumphant about this. She didn't explain to Susan that Pat's copy would also serve as evidence that Susan was satisfied with Pat's work, so Susan couldn't later claim that Pat had thrown things out against Susan's will. Pat herself had never had a client make such a claim, but some of her colleagues had. Better to learn from their misfortunes than to replicate them.

When noon rolled around, Pat suggested that because of the cold weather she would prefer to stay inside and eat lunch with Susan. Susan welcomed the idea and set about making a pot of Darjeeling.

Pat, wanting to keep the lunchtime conversation light and to indulge her own curiosity at the same time, ventured, "That's quite a nice car your neighbor owns."

"You mean the black sports car?"

"Uh-huh. The Porsche."

"He's there every Monday. He doesn't live there, you see. Isn't he handsome? I think he takes care of things for his aunt."

"You mean she lives there?"

"Yeah, I think so. Isn't he good looking?" Susan repeated.

"I only just caught a glimpse of him last week. Yes, I would have to call him gorgeous. You say his aunt?" As much as Pat wanted to discuss Rich, she did not want to seem overly interested in him. She was, after all, happily married. And she was, after all, here in a professional capacity, even if she had chosen to share lunch and tea with her client. "Have you ever met her?"

"Maybe it's his great aunt. I don't know for sure. I've never even seen her. I think she's housebound."

"Then how do you know it's his aunt? Have you met him?" Pat was able to ask this question quite innocently, even though it was getting at her real interest.

"Well, you see, sometimes in the summer he's there in the evening to mow her lawn. Can you imagine how great he looks in shorts and all glistening from the heat?" Pat was glad this was a rhetorical question. "Anyway, one time he came over to ask if he could borrow my phone. He explained the whole situation I'm sure, but, you see, I was struck so very brain-dead by his presence – like a silly schoolgirl with a crush – that I only remember fragments. I think he said his name was Henry something. And his aunt's phone was out of order and could he borrow mine to report the problem." Susan paused.

"Oh, Pat, I can tell you because you'll understand. The whole time he was talking all I could think was how I couldn't let him in the house because I couldn't let him – a vision of beauty and someone I would love to seem attractive to – I couldn't let him see the mess in my house! Thank goodness I had my cordless phone in my hand when I went to the door.

So I just offered it to him as naturally as I could, as if the thought of asking him in never even crossed my mind. So he made his call, handed me back the phone, and that was that. Of course, I haven't heard from him since."

Pat pulled herself together to make a professional comment, "Well, just think how happy you'll be next time he comes by and your house is all in order and you can invite him in." Then she returned to her more personal interest, "Would his last name be 'Landman'? That's what his license plate reads."

"I don't remember, you see. But, no, that doesn't sound right."

Pat and Susan finished their lunch in silence, both no doubt lost in their own reveries about Henry Rich Gorgeous Landman, or whatever his name was.

***

Thursday brought Susan's bubbly recap of her mini-reunion with Katie and Barb. It turned out that her friends had conspired, and Barb had actually flown in. Katie had picked her up at the airport on the way to lunch at Susan's. "Good thing I didn't know how to make a small pot of 'Sorority Stew', so we had plenty to eat!

"We had way plenty to drink, too. 'Stew and stewed' we used to call it back in college. I bet you can't guess what we decided to do with the dishes," Susan challenged.

Pat, the person, began thinking of things to guess. Pat, the professional, wondered if she was really meant to answer or should just declare she had no idea.

No matter, Susan just bubbled on, "We thought we should each keep one of the cups, so that every time we get together – and we agreed now we'll do it every year – every time we'll have to bring our cups for admission, to prove it's really us. Then, so no impostors can infiltrate, we smashed all the rest of the dishes into little pieces! You know, like when the Russians would make a toast and then throw their glasses into the fireplace." Susan paused and watched Pat closely. "Well, it seemed like a smashing idea at the time," she defended herself. "No pun intended," she fibbed with a smile.

"I'm so glad you had a good time." Pat genuinely meant it. "And that you gave your dishes a ceremonious send off," she concluded with her professional opinion.

***

Yes, by late Friday afternoon, Pat was feeling like her self-proclaimed title of most successful organizer in the State was well deserved.

Her client was making speedy, steady, and determined progress. The bedroom and kitchen were still in excellent shape. Susan had organized the bathroom completely on her own, after the jump-start with the small paper bag and the Internet cosmetic warnings. "All I kept were the two newest sets of nail polish, concealers, foundation, blush. And I bought one, just one, new tube of mascara to replace all the old ones," Susan had gestured expansively at the tiny room.

The garage was all set, except for the items that needed to be taken away and moved next Wednesday. The tool room in the basement was purged of anything rusty and everything else was sorted by category with multiples eliminated. Susan had discovered, with the help of some significant hints by Pat, that having a waste basket in every room really helped control clutter.

There had been serious deliberation over what piece of exercise equipment would be retained. "If you're really going to use a stationary bike, a treadmill, a stair machine, and this other contraption that looks like a torture device …"

"It's an ab strengthener," Susan had defended.

"… then you need to join a gym. There's just no justification for taking up this much living space with exercise equipment." Pat was adamant.

"But they each serve a different purpose, you see."

"Well, I'm afraid I don't quite see it as clearly as you seem to." Pat felt she must pursue this debate and was determined that her superior logic would win in the end. "There are basically three types of exercise – aerobic, weight-bearing, and stretching, right?"

"I guess so … yes."

"Okay. Now you don't have any stretching apparatus, do you?"

"Oh, do you recommend something?"

"No." This was not going well. "What I meant was we can divide what you have into two categories – aerobic and weight-bearing. So, aerobic-wise you have the bike, the treadmill, and the stair machine. Weight-wise you have the ab device, some free weights, and the stair machine."

"You listed the stair machine twice," Susan argued.

"That's because it falls in both categories. And it has a pretty small footprint. It would be a good choice."

"But, no! You see, it's the one I like the least. I only ever tried it once when I first got it. – Okay, I admit it was another late-night TV purchase. Great price; astronomical shipping! – I don't ... won't use it!"

"That's fine. A good choice logically, a bad choice psychologically. It's out of here." Pat flipped her thumb toward the garage door. "Which do you prefer, the bike or the treadmill? If I said you had to use one of them for fifteen minutes right now, which would you choose?"

"The treadmill, no question. It's easier and quieter."

"So how about you keep the treadmill and the free weights?"

"What about the ab thing?"

"You can strengthen your abdominals doing sit-ups."

"I never do sit-ups."

"Do you use the ab thing? ... Ever?"

"Well, no."

"Okay, everything except the treadmill and weights goes. Don't forget to enter them into the donation software."

Susan submissively tapped away at the laptop. "They don't look like they're worth much."

"That's because lots of other people have them sitting around unused."

"But I paid a small fortune for them."

"Yeah, I know. So did everyone else."

Susan agreed with the decision, but could not let any piece go without five minutes use. Pat decided to be a sport and use each one for five minutes herself. The bike was indeed noisy; the stairstepper had a jerky motion – *why not just use the real steps?* – and Pat considered herself lucky to extricate herself from the abster in one piece. No wonder no one used these things. Pat was happy she had tried them all – the experience would no doubt help her write a more authentic chapter in her book. She would have to make out an index card as soon as she was headed home.

It was a physical struggle to get the discarded machines anywhere near the door. "How did you ever get these in here?"

"I sweet-talked the delivery men, you see."

They left the wrestling of the treadmill into the spare bedroom for the movers.

"We're doing great!" Pat pronounced with some self-satisfaction. "All that's left is the living-dining room, your new office, and the second floor storage room."

"So, do I have any homework for the weekend?"

Pat wasn't sure if Susan was eager for homework or for a free weekend. But the assignment she had in mind should be a pleasant one. "Yes, I think you should set up the aquarium in your office." Susan smiled. "And then on Monday, we'll tackle that storage closet."

"Oh, don't tell me that."

"Tell you what?" Pat shot back as she gave Susan a wave goodbye and headed out to her minivan. "Have a good weekend!"

Chapter 12

Monday morning of Week Three, Pat found herself once again sitting and staring in Susan's driveway.

She had already indulged herself with a few minutes eyeing Rich's car, still looking newly polished with its sleek "LANDMAN" rear end. And she had conjured a very respectable daydream for herself – she owned her own sexy black Porsche convertible, and she was zipping along a country road on a sunny fall day, top down, with Fred by her side and the wind swirling around them. As her mind wandered, Rich came out of the house and snapped her back to reality. She didn't want him to see her staring in his direction. This time he was wearing, not carrying, his topcoat and a Burberry muffler – Pat would have ordinarily called it a scarf, but on Rich the word muffler just seemed more appropriate. What was it about a good looking rich guy with a fancy sports car that made a woman's heart flutter?

As he zoomed away, Pat turned her eyes toward Susan's house. And there she found another reason to stare. The bushes around the front door and the picture window were all neatly trimmed back, creating the inviting frame which had been their original purpose. Pat had no idea how Susan could have managed to do this, what with the snowpack and icy cold weather. She wondered if she could find a diplomatic way to ask. The trimming itself was evidence that Susan was feeling proud and confident of her organizing progress. Pat knew that it was best not to point this out, since it was likely that Susan had not given the psychology of the action any thought. *But, I know. How wonderful.*

Pat hopped out of her minivan and went around to the hatch to get the collapsible cardboard boxes she had brought to help with the day's project.

Between the glimpse of Rich and the bushes, Pat was raring to go.

"Well, first things first," began Pat. "Let me see your new fish!"

"They're very organized, you see! No clutter … just one underwater castle to swim around and some nice, natural, environmentally friendly pebbles. And to make it easy on myself I only got two fish. Very streamlined, a reflection of the new me!" Maybe Susan did understand about the bushes.

With show and tell over, it was time to get back to work. Susan was still dubious about attacking the storage closet. "Whenever you feel unsure of how to take the next step, you should look back at your plan." Pat pulled her notepad out of her case. "See, we've already figured it out, mostly. We'll sort through all the things and find them homes – here or elsewhere – the same way we did in the other rooms. The holiday decorations will go to the basement, on shelves where you can get at them easily. And for the paperwork, which you'll be tackling between now and the big payday, we'll put it in these bankers boxes I brought."

"It'll take me all day just to assemble those boxes,"

sighed Susan.

Susan's eyes widened as Pat pulled out one of the boxes and flipped, folded, and tucked both the box and its lid into shape in about thirty seconds. "I've had a lot of practice."

Much of the paperwork had been stuffed into shopping bags and stashed away on various occasions when Susan had been preparing for company. *Very typical.* That made it easy to box up and label with approximate dates. Susan spotted quite a few old catalogs that she immediately pitched. "Three weeks ago, I don't think I would have realized I could just do that!" School papers were easy to label with dates, as well.

There were a lot of odds and ends, too. Vases and baskets, staplers and rulers, jigsaw puzzles and a badminton set. Most of it was slated for St. Smith's. Some of it – like the old tennis balls – was trash. "Oh, wow! My pearl necklace! I knew it had to be somewhere!" Susan quickly fastened it around her neck. "That'll go in my bedroom." They also found two boxes of Susan's childhood toys. She wanted to keep them, so there was no need to go through them since they were already stored well.

The holiday decorations needed to be culled.

"I see you have six cartons of colored Easter egg shells," Pat observed. She had started to say, "Why do you have …?" but she caught herself and changed to the more nonjudgmental statement. "Some of them have become homes to little worms," she added matter-of-factly.

"Yeah, they were so pretty, you see, that I didn't want to throw them out."

"Yes, but some things aren't meant to be kept. Eggshells, even when they're dyed really pretty, are one of them. Sort of like you wouldn't keep a pretty paper plate after you ate birthday cake off of it."

"You're right. And besides, coloring the eggs is half the fun." Susan really was catching on.

Six more bags of trash made it to the curb in time for the Monday afternoon trash collection.

By the end of the day, the storage closet contained three boxes of memorabilia, fourteen boxes of paperwork to be gone through at a later date, and a significant amount of air. The former Wall of Food in the basement was now the Holiday Wall with a large box for each of New Years, Easter, Thanksgiving, Birthdays, Showers (bridal and baby), and

Patriotic Holidays. Halloween required two boxes, one with decorations and one with costume props. Valentine's Day, St. Patrick's Day, and Mardi Gras only required a shoebox each. Christmas – the biggie – needed six boxes, plus the carton containing the tree that had been stuffed into Susan's car trunk.

***

Pat and Susan spent Tuesday on a scavenger hunt through the living-dining room and the large spare bedroom to make sure they collected as much as possible for the charity pickups on Wednesday. When they had moved most of the old computer components out of the spare room, Susan gave a little gasp, and half whispered, "Pat, we've unearthed the weight machine. We forgot all about it when we were deciding on exercise equipment."

"Well, we won't need to spend five minutes each lifting weights," Pat chuckled as she quickly assessed the situation. "We'll get more than enough exercise taking this thing piece by piece into the living room so the Upward House people can take it away!"

"I wish the movers were coming today instead of Thursday!"

"Yes, well, sometimes even professional organizers

get the cart before the horse."

Susan, who was learning to plan ahead quite nicely, decided she had better call both St. Smith's and Upward House and tell them they should send a big truck because the pickup was substantial.

***

When Pat arrived on Thursday, the huge piles of boxes with their many items and the big pieces as well, all of which Susan had carefully entered into the donations software program, were gone. And soon the movers arrived, effortlessly carrying the treadmill into the guest room and the rolltop desk into the office.

Pat and Susan spent the rest of the morning sorting and shelving books, sorting and filing papers, and going through the remainder of the items that still needed a home. Regrettably, another two bankers boxes of papers had to be moved to the storage closet.

"Let's break for lunch. I think we'll make it extra long today so that after you eat you can take your car and get it washed. Then you can park it in the garage. Another triumphant milestone. Then we'll come up with our final pre-Dr. Hellen strategy while we enjoy our tea." Pat purposely used Dr. Hellen's name and the word "enjoy" in the same sentence, hoping to at least temporarily smooth down Susan's rough attitude about her sister.

"She better be satisfied," Susan sounded threatening. Pat hoped the tone would be better after lunch. Even though things appeared to be going smoothly, Pat had a sense that she was going to experience more than a little stress before the week was out. She decided to take advantage of the long lunch hour and indulge herself in a cheeseburger and fries. *Patience, Patience.*

***

The clean car in the garage had helped Susan's mood. And the cheeseburger – unbeknownst to Susan – had helped Pat's mood.

"Here's what I propose," began Pat, as she took a long sip of the rich Darjeeling and secretly wished she could just curl up with a good book. Instead, she took out her notepad to emphasize the weight of the plan. "This afternoon we'll set up your rolltop desk with a good system for handling your paperwork. Then tomorrow morning we'll devote to final staging for your sister's visit."

"I'm concerned about the four bags of trash in the living room." Pat wasn't sure if Susan was responding to Pat or just expressing her own unrelated thoughts.

"Well, I'll make an exception to my usual procedures and take them home with me." Reassurance was definitely what was being called for. Pat continued with her plan, "We'll get everything all set and take a run-through so you'll be at ease when your sister arrives. Maybe you should start your visit with one of these delicious pots of tea." Pat was trying so hard to convey a vision of a visit filled with mutual sisterly love.

"Well, you'll be here, too." It was a statement, not a question.

"Oh, you don't want me around as a third wheel."

"You're not an extra wheel, you're essential."

"Your sister doesn't even know I exist. And that's the way you said you wanted it."

"We'll tell her who you are; we just won't tell her what you are, you see." There was that deceit thing again that gave Pat the uneasy feeling.

"Are you sure?" One last feeble attempt to get out of what was sure to be a sticky situation.

"I'm positive. If you aren't here, I won't be either." Pat understood that Susan did not want to, and would not, be alone with her sister. *Crud!*

Chapter 13

Pat arrived at Susan's on Friday morning with a bouquet of pink and white carnations which she thought would add a polished touch to the kitchen table. She wanted the house to look homey and inviting, not organized to the point of sterility.

She and Susan spent the morning wandering from room to room trying to spot anything that might cause Dr. Hellen to declare the house unfit for the $100,000 reward.

"Do you think she'll open the upstairs storage hatch?" Susan fretted. "What if she thinks I should have sorted all those bankers boxes full of papers?"

"They're all categorized and labeled." That was the best Pat could say about them, but she expressed her opinion that Hellen should be satisfied, since they all looked neat and clean.

"I'll tell her they're my archives," Susan concluded. Pat did not want to affirmatively endorse this exaggeration, so she kept quiet.

After lunch Pat parked her minivan a couple houses down the street. She didn't want Hellen to see the "hire a professional organizer" license plate frame on a vehicle sitting in Susan's driveway. She couldn't cover it, so she hoped it would go unnoticed on the street.

Two o'clock arrived and there was no sign of Hellen. Two-o-five, and Susan was getting fidgety. "Why don't you start a pot of tea?" Pat figured it would give Susan something to do. Susan filled the kettle and turned on the heat. At two-o-eight, the doorbell rang. Pat sat on the living room couch while Susan went to the door.

"I didn't see your car. I thought maybe you weren't home." Hellen's greeting was true to form.

"It's in the garage." There were hints of both triumph and defiance in Susan's response.

"Who's this?" Hellen had noticed Pat.

"This is Pat." Susan pretended not to notice Hellen's rudeness. Pat crossed the room quickly and shook Hellen's hand firmly as she looked her square in the eye. "You see, she's my financial advisor." Pat was not ready for this grossly stretched designation, but she had no choice but to smile politely.

"A banker with a financial advisor?! Ha!" Just who had failed to teach Hellen any manners?

Susan was determined. "Don't some psychiatrists have psychiatrists, too?" Pat caught the undertone here even if it was lost on Hellen.

The tea kettle started to whistle. "You two go ahead with what you're doing. I'll finish making the tea," Pat concluded. Susan shot her a look that said "you can't leave me alone with her!" but Pat did not see how a financial advisor could insert herself into a tour of her client's house. The way she saw it, Susan had backed herself into this one.

Susan and Hellen headed upstairs; Pat went into the kitchen. She could overhear a few snippets of conversation.

"When did you get the new bedroom set?"

"I've had it all along."

"I would have thought this would have been crammed full." Apparently the storage hatch met with approval.

Susan and Hellen went by Pat on their way to the basement and garage. Pat briefly considered what it would be like having Hellen stay for tea. Surely it would not be pleasant. Pat didn't need to worry, though, as Hellen was soon hurrying back up the steps and through the kitchen. "It looks incredible. Keep it this way for six months and the money's yours. I doubt you can do it, though. Ha!" And as she passed Pat, "Don't waste your time on any elaborate financial plans." Then she was out the door.

The whole Hellen event had been rather like some doctor visits – much dreaded, not really pleasant, and over rather quickly. Pat and Susan drank their tea in silence.

Finally, Pat found her professional self. "That went very well, as well as we could have expected." And she suggested that she come to work with Susan again on the third Monday of February, which Susan would have off from work because it was a bank holiday.

Susan agreed and gushed over how she never could have done any of this without Pat. There were heartfelt hugs, a few tears from Susan, and then Pat departed. She stopped around the corner to phone Fred with the news of success. Then she drove home, back to her own small mess over which no one but she would pass judgment.

Chapter 14

It was five-thirty on a Friday evening in early February. It was dark. It was cold. It was sleeting. Pat was squinting to see where she needed to turn in order to get to the back parking lot of the bank hosting the after-hours business networking mixer. Pat saw the value of these events, but she didn't really enjoy them. Every now and then, such as tonight, the chamber of commerce would hold one where the member and a guest could attend for free. She would tell Fred and he would be a sport and agree to meet her there when he got off work. They would eat cold pizza, pedestrian sushi, or a piece of the giant submarine sandwich, drink a glass or two of wine, and call it dinner. If it weren't for Fred's support, Pat would never have come out on a night like this.

Now, as Pat pulled behind the building and began looking for a spot, she could see the yellow blinking lights of a tow truck near the building's back entrance. Thank goodness she didn't have a dead battery, flat tire, or whatever!

She parked the car, checked to make sure she had her nametag, and headed for the door. As she got close, she looked to see if she knew the owner of the ailing vehicle. And there was the shiny black Porsche 911 she had admired those three Monday mornings she had gone to Susan's. It was minutes from being rudely hoisted by the tow truck's winch and carted away. Rich Gorgeous was nowhere in sight.

Without really thinking, Pat hurried inside, gave a dismissive wave to the person at the registration table, scanned the networking crowd, and spotted Rich. She ran right up, didn't even excuse herself for interrupting his conversation, and blurted, "Your car is about to be towed!"

"Excuse me?"

"You parked your car in a handicapped spot, and it's about to be towed!" Pat wondered why he didn't see the urgency. She assumed he didn't realize his mistake, that in the dark and sleet he had not seen the tiny blue sign that indicated the parking restriction.

"There must be some mistake." Of course Rich didn't recognize Pat and he must have thought she was crazy.

"Black Porsche 911, license plate 'Landman'?" Pat wanted to be sure Rich saw the folly of his delay.

"Yes, but I'm entitled to park there." Rich replied matter-of-factly, while at the same time processing what Pat had said and sprinting toward the door.

Pat was extremely disappointed. Here was a beautiful physical specimen of a man– so much so that, in Pat's mind, she had practically elevated him to the status of a demigod – and wealthy besides, and it turned out that he was pompous and self-centered. Entitled, indeed! She should have minded her own business and let them tow his precious car.

Pat walked over to the bar and ordered a glass of Merlot. She took a sip and scanned the room for someone to talk with. She saw Rich come back in.

He walked over to her and said, "Thanks so much. I got it taken care of." Then, "I would introduce myself, but apparently we've met. I'm so sorry I don't remember your name."

Just then, Susan walked up. "Hi, Pat." Of course she would be here; it was her bank hosting the event. Pat really had nothing nice to say to Rich, so she said, "Hi, Susan. Great timing. There's someone I want you to meet." Susan recognized Rich and fixed Pat with a look somewhere between exhilaration and bewilderment. *What had Susan said Rich's real name was? Henry!* "Henry, this is Susan Huffman, she's the branch manager here at the bank. Susan, this is Henry." Pat said it as if there was no need for Henry to have a last name. Then, "Oh, I see my husband just came in. Sorry, gotta go." And she made her escape.

Pat grabbed Fred's hand and steered him to the bar. He got his glass of wine and she pulled him aside, giving him a brief account of what had just happened. "Can you believe the nerve!?"

"Maybe you misunderstood the situation," Fred said calmly as he swirled and sipped his wine. "This isn't too bad for the price," he assessed.

"I don't think so!" came back Pat. Then, in response to Fred's quizzical look, "About the situation, not the wine."

"Maybe he really is handicapped," Fred continued to advocate for Rich.

"He looks fine to me!"

"How can you tell? You can't see much of him in that business suit."

"Susan saw him last summer in nothing but shorts and said he looked fabulous."

"Well, perhaps he has a glass eye," Fred would not give up.

Neither would Pat. "I was talking to him up close and his eyes looked fine to me," she huffed. "I think he's just one of those stuck-up guys who thinks he's entitled to break the rules because he has money."

"Maybe it's a heart condition."

"Yeah, right." It was just not fun to have one's fantasies ruined by reality.

Fred chuckled and teased, "Okay, then have it your way. The way I see it, you got what you deserved for admiring another man!" Pat shot him her best dagger-eyed look, but Fred had got the last word.

Chapter 15

When Pat received an email from Susan canceling their Monday bank holiday appointment because Susan was getting together with Katie, Pat didn't even care. The thrill of catching another glimpse of Rich Gorgeous had been displaced by a total disdain of Henry the Arrogant. Pat merely sent Susan a reply wishing her a pleasant time with Katie and suggesting that Susan call at her convenience to reschedule.

And now that the previously appointed Monday had arrived, Pat was particularly glad about the cancellation. The temperature was in the teens and a steady snow was falling and accumulating. Pat decided to spend the day working on an article for her website.

First she built a roaring fire in the fireplace. Then she brewed a strong cup of very hot tea. And now she sat, laptop at the ready, staring out the window at the falling snow and wondering what to write about. This was one of the burdens of keeping up the image of the most successful organizer in the State. Every month Pat had to write a new and informative essay on an interesting organizing topic. It was important that the website's content be fresh and compelling in case big publicity hit or a highly influential personality took note. But it was hard to get really excited when only a couple hundred people would read the article. That's about the amount of traffic the website was getting according to Pat's webmaster, a high school student who lived a couple doors down the street. Still, one never knew if one of those two hundred people would be worth a lot of business. Besides, Pat figured that, at some point, she could compile all of the articles, and then she'd have another – or the first – book to her credit.

Pat sat down her cup, pulled the computer onto

her lap, and looked at the blank document. Absentmindedly, she picked up a rubber band and began twiddling it on her fingers. Blank, blank was her mind; twiddle, twiddle went her fingers; crackle, crackle went the fire. Blank, blank, twiddle, twiddle, crackle, crackle. Blank, twiddle, crackle, blank …. Then, snap! The rubber band broke and stung the back of Pat's hand bringing her back to the wordless document. She rubbed the offended hand, took a long sip of her tea, and picked up the rubber strip. Holding one end in each hand, she stretched it out and looked at it with much greater intensity than it would receive any other time than on a lazy day in front of a glowing fire. She examined the little nicks along the sides of the rubber band and recognized that it could have broken in any number of places. And that was all she needed to launch her article.

An hour later, Pat had written a creative essay on desk supplies and how they could clutter up a person's workspace. Starting with rubber bands, she explained how rubber turns brittle over time – hadn't the readers all experienced finding the calcified shards of an old rubber band at the bottom of a desk drawer? Yet, rubber bands were sold in such large quantities; unless a project called for using a great number at once, wouldn't a significant portion of a purchased package be doomed to spoilage? But, rubber bands also arrive from many free sources – around a diverse assortment of things from bundled mail to fresh vegetables. If a person just collected the clean, elastic bands that happened their way, wouldn't they have enough? And couldn't the same be said for paperclips? These days office supply stores seemed to sell them in packs of 1,000 for about a dollar. But did anyone really need 1,000 paperclips? Using the same theory as the "take a penny, leave a penny" trays next to cash registers, wouldn't a little pile of fifteen or twenty paperclips per desk be enough to exist in perpetuity? Staples, of course, didn't pose quite the same problems since they weren't reusable. Although, they did tend to be sold 5,000 at a time. So, one should resist the temptation to add a dollar's worth of staples to every office supply order. It's these little things, concluded Pat, that can bog down the efficiency of a workstation.

Pat attached her masterpiece to an email and sent it off to David, the high school student webmaster down the street, for uploading to her site.

Then she added a log to the fire, poked around at it for a few minutes for good measure, traded her teacup for two wine glasses and a bottle of Pinot Noir that would be great with the salmon at dinner, collected the day's mail to review, and settled back in to await Fred's arrival home from work.

* * *

A couple weeks went by and Pat had still not heard back from Susan. So Pat sent her another email:

<Please let me know when you have time to schedule our next meeting.>

She received a reply almost immediately:

<Very busy schedule right now. But I've been going through the boxes of old papers in the storage hatch. What was in the first four boxes now just takes up two. Thanks.>

Pat wondered briefly how Susan had found time to go through the boxes if her schedule was so tight. But she also marveled at Susan's self-motivation. If only all – or half – of her clients had so much persistence! She responded:

<Great! Keep up the good work! And let me know when you catch a break in your schedule.>

***

Pat got busy with other things – coordinating the reverse raffle for her favorite charity's annual fundraiser, planning the summer's front-yard flower bed and backyard vegetable patch, designing the storage space for a client's kitchen remodeling project, setting up an office for a home-based business client, and collecting more index cards full of ideas for her book.

It was the end of April before Pat realized she had not heard back from Susan. Once Susan was back in her thoughts, Pat became concerned. She sent Susan another email:

<We should really get together to assess how your systems are working while we still have time to make sure everything will be in order for your sister's visit.>

Pat really hated even to allude to Dr. Hellen, but she felt it was necessary. She tried to make it sound as non-threatening as possible.

The next morning, she had Susan's reply:

<Don't worry. Everything is in order. Hellen is coming at 10:00 AM on July 21, so please plan to be here.>

It was still pretty early in the morning, so Pat picked up the phone and dialed Susan's number. After four rings, she got the answering machine. Susan must have left for work early. Pat left a brief message, "Hi Susan, it's Pat Oaktree. I really think we should get together at least briefly sometime in the next couple of weeks. Please give me a call. Thanks. Bye."

Susan did not call back. Instead, late that evening, she sent another email:

<Hi, Pat. Sorry it got too late for me to call. But, don't give it another thought. Everything is fine, and I'll see you on July 21.>

Pat thought hard. Had she done something to offend Susan? The last she had spoken with her was at that networking event at the bank. Susan had come over to Pat and Fred as they were nibbling little eggrolls and drinking their wine. Pat had introduced Susan as the branch manager, not wanting Susan to think that Pat shared confidential client information even with Fred. Susan had been gracious, and even thanked Pat for introducing her to Henry, indicating that he might be a valuable business client. Pat had been glad that Susan hadn't expressed or required any praise of Henry on a personal level.

No, Pat couldn't think of anything she had done that might have upset Susan. And Susan had always been very up-front with Pat. If Susan said she was too busy to meet and everything was still in order, then Pat believed her.

Pat circled July 21 boldly on her calendar, and for now, workwise, that's all that mattered. Summer was just around the corner. Pat and Fred's son and daughter would both be home from college. Pat would be busy with extra cooking and laundry, reading some good summertime fiction, and trying to care that she had a business to run, a book to write, and her self-proclaimed reputation as the most successful organizer in the State to maintain.

Chapter 16

Charlene and Benjamin arrived home for the summer within hours of each other. Charley brought her stuff in through the back door, and the family room became a sea of boxes, suitcases, and small pieces of furniture. Ben, who arrived second, had to come in through the front door and quickly filled the living room. Pat surveyed the situation front and back. *If my clients saw this house now, they would never hire me.* How many times had Pat told people that being clutter-free did not necessarily mean one was organized and that a lack of neatness did not necessarily mean a person was disorganized. Here was a perfect case in point. Her family was merely in transition. And, while she was sure that, if asked, her clients would guess that the first thing Pat would require was that all of this stuff be put in its proper place, they would be wrong. Fred had taken the day off, Pat had baked a double batch of chocolate chip cookies, and everyone sat down at the dining room table for cookies, milk, and catching up.

Charley, Pat's born-organized child, had mounted a systematic employment search via email and landed a summer data entry job at the nearby community college. Ben, Pat had to admit, was borderline chronically disorganized, not unlike Pat herself. He was at a loss when it came to how he would spend his summer.

"How about if I get you a job unpacking executives being relocated to the City by their employers?" Pat offered.

"I wouldn't know what to do!" Ben inclined his head and eyes toward his own newly moved piles.

"I could go with you on the first job and train you." Pat had done this kind of work for a couple years when she had first started her professional organizing business.

"It sounds like hard work." Now Ben was sounding lazy.

"Yes, but it pays quite well." Pat knew what would motivate him.

"Well, I can give it a try if you can get me the job."

***

A week later, Pat and Ben were off to a "corporate executive unpack."

Pat was driving; Ben was navigating using the computer-generated map and directions. "It'll take us almost an hour to get there! Do we get paid for that?"

"We get paid half the hourly rate for travel."

"Wow!"

"But we have to pay for the gas."

"We still come out ahead." So far, Ben was liking this.

"This email we got with the assignment says the shipment is 21,400 pounds! That's more than ten tons! That can't be right, can it?"

"Oh, yes," Pat affirmed. "People have a lot of stuff. And when someone else is paying for the move, they don't think twice about having it all go with them."

"No wonder you can stay in business," Ben mused.

He was silent for a minute or two, thinking about what his mother had just said. Then he said with concern, "We have to put it all away, right? How long do we get to do that?"

"Since there are two of us, we should be able to get it all done today. When you go out on your own, you'll usually spend two days. Don't forget, furniture is heavy, so that counts for a lot of the weight, and you don't have to do anything with it. That's handled by the movers."

"Uh-huh." Ben tipped his head back and closed his eyes.

***

The new executive residence of the Tatem family was a massive recently constructed house in an upscale suburban development. Pat did not prefer this type of home. In her mind, some of the rooms were too large – who needed a bathroom with enough floor space for a king-size bed? That just meant more time needed to keep it clean. And some of the rooms were way too small – the dining rooms were often no larger than the bathrooms. Didn't anybody sit down to a meal with family and friends anymore? Pat could go on; she didn't like the layout, the functionality, or the construction – plastic trim instead of woodwork. For the same amount of money, a person could buy a grand old mansion – with real plaster walls – in Pat's community. But the developers courted the real estate agents who in turn pushed these homes to out-of-town transfers – after all, who would want old craftsmanship when you could have brand-new construction?

And landscaping? The entire development had been clearcut. Now the only trees were newly planted saplings. The sod in the front lawn was yet to be unrolled. *Patience! Snap out of it!*

The movers were still unloading the last of the boxes, and the front door was wide open. Pat and Ben rang the bell as a formality, then walked in with Pat calling, "Ms. Tatem? Ms. Tatem?"

A woman, in her late thirties, maybe forty, came down the stairway with a preteen girl following behind. "I'm Alice Tatem." She didn't look like she had been expecting anyone.

"I'm Pat, and this is Ben. We're here to get you unpacked and organized."

"Oh, yes. They said they were sending someone. Well, I guess you know what to do. I have to take Jess over to the school for some placement testing." Alice gave Pat the impression that she was on her way out the door.

"Could you maybe show us around so we know the general purpose of your rooms?" Pat asked hopefully.

"You're the experts. I think you'll find it self-explanatory. The furniture's all in the right rooms, and most of the boxes, too." And just like that, they were gone.

Ben looked at Pat. "How can she leave her house wide open and all her stuff – packed and ready to go – with total strangers?"

"People and their stuff," replied Pat. "You never know from one person to the next."

Pat and Ben gave themselves a tour of the house. They concluded that Jess was an only child. They locked the doors after the movers finished and got down to business.

"We'll start in the kitchen and then move to the bedrooms. Those are the areas most people want done first."

Pat showed Ben how to unwrap the dishes from the mover's craft paper. "Be very careful, sometimes a tiny piece will be all wrapped up in ten sheets of paper. And flatten all the paper – that way you know you got everything, plus it's easier to throw out."

Ben opened a carton. "These glasses are all covered in grease and dust," he said with disgust.

"They probably haven't been used in years. Packers start at the front of a cabinet and work to the back, so the stuff on top is the stuff that was buried the deepest."

"Do we have to wash them?"

"Ideally, but we don't have time. Put them in the back and Alice probably won't use them the whole time she lives here. She probably doesn't even remember she owns them. I once had a lady swear I was unpacking someone else's crate until I pulled out something from all the way down in the bottom and she exclaimed, 'Oh, now that's mine!'"

***

When they got to the bedroom, Pat set aside everything that would go in dresser drawers. "That stuff's generally too personal for us to handle," she said, and moved on to the closet.

"This closet is as big as my bedroom!" Ben was

amazed. "In fact, I think it's bigger than my dorm room!"

There were ten wardrobe packs, and it turned out that nine of them were filled with sweatshirts. Sweatshirts from all over the world – Naples, Rome, and Paris; Cairo, Tel Aviv, and Kingston; Rio, Santiago, and Panama City; Hong Kong and Taipei; Disneyland, Disney World, Yellowstone, and Yosemite. At least 200 sweatshirts!

"These people have been everywhere!" Ben said enviously.

"It's an impressive collection," Pat admitted, "but postcards would have taken less space."

"Yeah, but, Mom, you can't wear postcards! This way everyone who sees you knows where you've been!"

***

When Alice and Jess returned later in the day, Pat had Ben give them a tour of the work. When they arrived at the bedroom closet, Pat said, "This is quite a collection of sweatshirts you have!"

"Yes, we pick one up everyplace we travel," Alice proudly stated the obvious. "I wish we had some way to display them. But they take up so much room."

Postcards. If you were my client, I would suggest you switch to collecting postcards. "You'll have to wear a different one every cool day of the year," Pat offered lightheartedly.

***

On the way home, Ben admitted that he was exhausted. But when he learned that he would only have one or two unpacking jobs a week and he would make more money than Charley would working forty-five hours a week, he decided it was a pretty sweet deal.

"Well, it works for a summer job," Pat tried to sound parental. She was glad that Ben was happy.

Chapter 17

July 21 arrived without a word from Susan. At nine-thirty Pat noted the somewhat more disorderly state of her own house – Ben still had a couple boxes in the living room – jiggled the doorknob to make sure it was locked, and headed out for her appointment. She wondered if anyone would be there.

They were there. As Pat pulled up to park at the curb in front of Susan's house, she saw Dr. Hellen's car in the driveway. She hoped Susan would not be upset that Pat had not been there when Hellen had arrived. But it was still several minutes before ten; Pat could not be held responsible for Hellen's early arrival.

Pat took a minute to look for telltale signs of backsliding. She found none. The draperies and curtains were open, the bushes were neatly trimmed. To Pat's delight, Susan had even planted flowers in the beds and along the walk. *This could be my biggest success yet!* Pat could already taste the celebratory cup of tea Susan was sure to brew.

Pat picked up her case and grabbed the door handle to get out of the minivan. As she did so, she saw Dr. Hellen bolt down the two front steps. Hellen hopped into her car and roared away. If Pat had stepped out of the minivan, Hellen would have run her over.

Pat walked up to the door. Susan was standing just inside, sobbing. "I'm so sorry. You see, she's just awful. I'm so sorry. So sorry."

"I guess maybe you should have let me come a few times since January." Pat was not feeling sympathetic. Susan continued to sob. Pat softened a little, "What didn't meet with her approval?"

"Nothing. I mean, everything was in perfect order. Take a look for yourself." Susan slumped down into the rocking chair and waved her hand in a dismissive way. Pat realized that Susan literally meant for Pat to inspect the house. And so she did.

And Susan was right. Everything was even better than when Pat had last seen it. There were only six boxes left in the storage hatch. Nothing had slid back into excess or disarray. What could have possibly gone wrong? Pat completed her circuit back to the living room and sat down on the couch opposite Susan.

"Susan, the place looks fantastic!" Pat was doing her best to avoid thinking about what all of this meant about her share of the payoff. "What did Hellen say?"

"She said ... she said it was incredible, she couldn't believe her eyes." Susan sobbed. Pat waited. "Then I hinted at the money, and she got all self-righteous and said I shouldn't be so greedy ... that getting my life in order should be payoff enough. Then ... then she said – oh, I can't stand her! – she said that she was happy to have helped. And before I could say another word, she left!"

"In a way, I suppose she's right." Pat was really acting now. She had known all along that this job had been risky, but she wasn't prepared for this. "But," she continued, to show she was on Susan's side, "it wasn't the deal."

"Now I can't pay you." Susan blurted it out as if she couldn't stand to let it go unsaid any longer.

"Well, maybe we can work something out." Pat's mind raced. "Maybe you would be willing to pay me the extra money you'll save on your income tax from all the charitable deductions." Pat figured that would run well into the thousands of dollars.

"That won't work, either." Susan broke into another wave of sobs. "I don't have any income to deduct from."

"I don't understand."

"You see, I lost my job back in February. I decided to just take the rest of the year off, because I knew I'd be netting seventy-five thousand dollars from the deal with Hellen. I just took the time and finished sorting through everything. It seemed like such a good plan. And I thought you'd be impressed, too."

Well, that explained it – why Susan had been so evasive, how she had made so much progress, and why Pat was getting nothing. Pat felt sick.

"I see." Pat knew she had to keep her cool, be professional. And she knew she couldn't do it for much longer. "That is unfortunate," Pat heard her own voice sounding flat. She took a deep breath.

"We'll probably both be better off if I just leave now."

Susan did not respond. Pat left.

***

Pat got into her minivan. Fred was in an editorial board meeting and could not be reached. Pat started toward home. Her mind was racing and numb at the same time. It was too early in the day for a cheeseburger. There had been no tea at Susan's. Pat pulled into the nearest coffee emporium, ordered an extra large double mocha mud beverage, and slumped into a seat.

She took a sip. She forced herself to focus on what had just happened, on analyzing what had gone wrong. What could she have done differently? Given the situation she had accepted when she took Susan on as a client, Pat couldn't think of anything that she could have done that would have changed the outcome.

Pat thought about calling her trusted colleague five states over, the one she always called when presented with sticky professional issues. But Pat didn't want to ruin the illusion of her being successful, and she couldn't figure a way to spin her current situation right now while she still felt so bitter.

Pat knew that some organizers required written contracts with their clients. But Pat couldn't see how that would have helped either. The contract would have been with Susan. And, Pat had to be fair, Susan had more than held up her end of the bargain. In fact, Susan genuinely seemed to want to pay Pat. And no contract in the world would amount to anything if Susan didn't have any money to pay.

Pat sighed, took another sip, and let her mind drift.

She watched as the barista took her grease pen and wrote the orders on the paper coffee cups. Whir, whir – the beans were ground. Tamp, tamp – the ground beans were pressed into the strainers. Hiss, hiss and drip, drip – the espresso brewed. Meanwhile, the barista poured the milk into the steamer and turned it on. She added the flavor shots to the cup. She took her grease pen and marked the next order on the next cup. She poured the espresso into the first cup. Whir, whir – the next set of beans was ground. Beep – the milk was steamed. She poured it into the first cup, placed a lid on it, and called out the order. Bang, bang – she emptied the grounds from the strainers. Tamp, tamp – the ground beans were pressed into the strainers ….

A perfect model of efficiency. No wasted motions – the quickest, most accurate result delivered to the customer. Total consistency of quality. A professional organizer's dream.

Yes, thought Pat, others had their theories about why coffee emporia were so popular. There was the one about there being more telecommuters and home-based business owners who needed an inexpensive place to hold meetings. There was the one about the economy being bad so people turned from large luxuries to small ones.

But Pat had her own theory. People were too disorganized. Their time management was not good, and they were sleep deprived. They would enter the coffee emporium and a number of their needs were met. A heavy dose of caffeine to keep them awake, plus a sense of attaining that elusive goal of order and efficiency as they watched the barista. For those who could stop to enjoy their beverage, the emporium was a small haven of peace in a harried world. And for those who could not even spare that much time, the to-go cup provided a means of carrying the dream with them.

And, had it not been thoroughly predictable, Pat's thoughts went on, that the popularity of those ultra-potent peppermints would follow? They cleaned away the coffee breath, soothed the stomach upset from the extra acid, and gave an additional mental boost at the same time.

You could get organized. Or you could turn to caffeine and peppermint. Surely this would make a good topic for a future article on Pat's website.

Da-doot. Da-doot. Pat's cell phone rang with Fred's special ringtone. She gave him a brief version of the Susan story.

"Well then, I'll take you out for a steak dinner tonight. You need it. And you deserve it. I love you. Ppch!"

Really, Pat shouldn't complain.

***

But, as Pat and Fred nibbled their salads and sipped their Cabernet, Pat did complain.

"You should be happy," Fred replied. "You did a great thing for Susan. You were a success. It's that Hellen who's the failure." Fred was Pat's biggest fan.

"But the deal was that if Susan succeeded, we'd get the money."

"Forget the money. You knew the whole thing was a gamble from the start."

"But I'm not running a charity, Fred."

"I know. But, I just want you to be happy."

Fred and steak always made Pat feel better. Together, they were irresistible.

Chapter 18

After the kids went back to school in the fall, Fred and Pat decided to take a long weekend and go to a little resort town in Canada. "Oop noorth," as Susan's brother Joe would say.

No matter how many times she went there, Pat was always fascinated by just how foreign Canada could seem for a neighboring place that primarily spoke English and transacted business in dollars and cents. Subtle differences in advertising, restaurant menus, street signage. Things were different here, and yet they were the same. Pat knew from her professional organizing acquaintances in Canada that the stresses of clutter and time were just as widespread for the people "oop noorth" as they were for those "doon sooth."

But Pat didn't want to think about that now. She and Fred had come here to escape from the stresses of their own life. They were here to relax. So, they had spent the afternoon meandering through antique stores. They had seen a great many interesting items – fortunately none of which they couldn't live without. And they had ended up here in the local beanery to rest their feet and partake of a recreational cup of coffee.

They sat down at a table overlooking the street. Fred pulled out the local newspaper, turned to the back pages, and began working on the crossword puzzle. Fred loved crossword puzzles, and he had been particularly enjoying the added challenges of the Canadian versions, with their different nuances and slang.

Pat preferred logic problems where all the information you needed for the solution was in front of you if you could just manipulate it the right way. She was content savoring her beverage and looking out the window. She was thinking about how cheery the street was with its colorful baskets of flowering plants hanging from every lamppost. There were five such posts visible from where Pat sat, two in front of the beanery and three across the street.

Pat was studying the flower baskets, the weave of the wire, and the Spanish moss that stuck out between it. She marveled at how healthy every single one of the plants looked. In the background she barely noticed a quiet whirring sound. If she thought about it at all, she thought it was a coffee grinder behind the counter at the back of the store. But then she became aware that the whirring sound was getting louder and that it was coming from outdoors. She inclined her head to try to get a better directional read on the sound and, as she did so, she saw the source pull into view from the right along the curb across the street.

There was a man in a wide-brimmed hat, standing on an elevated, walled platform, driving a most intriguing vehicle. Behind the driver's platform was a horizontal cylindrical tank. Pat would guess that it could hold about 150 gallons. The man stopped the contraption when he was just even with the first lamppost. He reached over and plucked a few spent blooms from the plant basket. Then he twirled the basket on its chain and did the same on the other side of the plant. Next, he grabbed a hose which Pat could see was connected to the tank, squeezed the trigger nozzle, and watered the plant. As he started the vehicle toward the next lamppost, a street sweeping mechanism at the very back neatly whisked up the debris which he had let fall to the ground. Another masterpiece of organization – a machine, designed for maximum efficiency, operated according to a schedule, to produce a consistent, desired result!

Pat turned to get Fred's attention so she could share her discovery with him. She saw that he was no longer working on the crossword puzzle. Instead, he was busy making his editor's marks on the feature article on the facing page.

Here they were, miles from home, on a getaway weekend, and yet, when left on their own, they had each been captivated by something related to their work. *How wonderful that we both so enjoy our careers!*

Chapter 19

The last of the trick-or-treaters had been treated. The candle in the jack-o-lantern had been extinguished. Fred lit the logs in the fireplace and Pat brewed a pot of tea so that they could each enjoy two of the four snack-size candy bars that remained.

Fred was reading the day's newspaper. Pat was opening the mail.

"Here's an engagement announcement you'll want to read. I believe you know the bride-to-be." Fred tossed a section of the paper toward Pat.

She read:

Huffman/Bennett

Ms. Susan Huffman, a former bank manager, announces her engagement to Mr. Henry Bennett III.

Mr. Bennett is the principal owner of a large privately held real estate development company. He is also a Purple Heart veteran, having lost the toes on his right foot in an explosion while serving in the Gulf War.

Ms. Huffman is the daughter of the late Mr. and Mrs. William Huffman. Mr. Bennett is the son of Mr. and Mrs. Henry Bennett II, the prominent philanthropists.

A December wedding is planned.

"Oh my goodness! He really is disabled!" Pat exclaimed.

"Huh?"

"The groom."

"I thought you knew the bride. Wasn't she your client? The one whose sister wouldn't pay up?"

"Yeah. But I know the groom, too. He's that guy with the Porsche. The one at the wine and cheese mixer who parked in the handicap spot and almost had his car towed."

"No way!"

"Yes, it's him. And it turns out he's a Purple Heart Veteran …. I feel awful."

"Why? You introduced them. Now you can add matchmaker to your list of accomplishments."

Pat reflected on the situation. Pat, who prided herself on being nonjudgmental. How could she have been so quick to judge – indeed, misjudge – Henry Bennett? Could it be that she was so careful not to judge her clients that she had become even more prone to judge others? Pat would have to watch against that. Could it be that she had subconsciously not wanted Rich Gorgeous to be as wonderful as he appeared, so she had jumped at the first hint of a possibility that he wasn't? Could it be …

"Are you going to send them something?" Fred

broke Pat's thoughts.

"Hardly!" Pat paused. How could she? She had ended her relationship with Susan in a professional manner, but certainly a bit on the cooler side. She would not want Susan to see a renewed contact as a reminder of debts unpaid. "No," Pat replied to Fred a second time in a more considered tone, "I don't think it would be appropriate."

If Pat were honest with herself, she was more than a little upset by the whole situation. Misjudgments aside, it just did not seem fair – although, of course, it was – for Susan to get both the guy and the money. Yes, Pat was heartwarmed to know that her professional expertise and her social interactions were responsible for Susan and Henry's happiness. But she was still a little miffed that she had gotten nothing personally to show for her efforts, that she was being forced by circumstances to be satisfied with the knowledge of a job more than well done.

Pat willed herself not to be bitter. She took a bite of her candy bar and concentrated on the chocolatey sweetness.

Chapter 20

It had been thirteen months since Pat first met Susan Huffman, and not much had changed. It was a cold February morning. Pat selected her boots from the pile of footwear just inside the door. As she pulled them on she looked back into the dining room where her teacup and crumpled paper napkin remained on the table. She pulled the door shut behind her, jiggled the knob to make sure it had locked, and headed toward the garage. *I should be staying home.*

Instead, Pat was headed to Susan's. Pat had been sitting at her desk a few days earlier when she had received the email from Susan:

\<Can you come by the house on Wednesday morning around 10:00? I have a small matter I'd like your help with.\>

Pat's first reaction was to write back, \<Sorry, I can't make it.\> But, Pat had a policy of not replying to emails with her first negative thoughts.

She started thinking. Her imagination let loose. She wondered why Susan would still be at her old house now that she was married to Henry. Perhaps the marriage had never happened. Maybe it had been very short-lived, and Susan had moved back to her old house and would pour out her whole tale of woe to Pat over a cup of that deliciously robust Darjeeling. No, it was probably something way more mundane.

Pat reread the email. Susan had said it was a small matter. That suggested something like rearranging a kitchen cabinet or archiving a few files. Pat wondered if Susan planned to pay her for her time. At this point, Pat didn't even care.

But, she was curious. She wanted to ask Susan a dozen questions. *Patience, Patience.* After a couple of hours, Pat emailed back a simple reply:

\<I'll see you then.\>

Now, it was familiar and strange at the same time as Pat drove up Susan's street. The old man with his routines was filling his bird feeders. The Christmas tree lady was putting up a Valentine's Day heart wreath on her door. Rich Gorgeous's – Henry's – Porsche was even parked in his aunt's driveway!

Pat realized there would be no fantastic stories over tea. In front of Susan's house was a moving van, and, as Pat parked her minivan on the street, she saw two husky movers carry the rolltop desk out the front door and up the truck ramp. Perhaps Susan needed some last-minute packing advice.

Pat rang the delightfully old-fashioned doorbell. Krrrriiiiing! Then she walked through the open door calling, "Hello! Susan?"

Susan appeared in front of her just as the movers came up from behind. "Hi, Pat. Hey, guys, you see, this is the organizer I was telling you about."

"Nice ta meet ya," said the first one. "You the lady who got all Sue's stuff in order? Unbelievable! Easiest packin' job we ever had!"

"Give them a bunch of your cards, Pat," Susan encouraged. "Maybe they can send you some referrals."

Pat reached into her case and pulled out a little rubber-banded packet of business cards. Maybe this was why Susan had invited her over. The mover stuffed them unceremoniously into a pocket of his overalls. "Yeah, thanks. There's a lotta people could use ya." He moved on toward the bedroom-turned-home-office.

"We're in the kitchen," Susan motioned Pat to follow her. Pat could see the house was almost completely empty. Henry was sitting on the kitchen counter. He looked as good as ever, dressed in a university sweatshirt and jeans. "You've met Henry, of course," Susan chirped. Well, actually, no, Pat never had met Henry. She had seen him, she had spoken with him, she had introduced him to Susan. But she had never actually met him. Pat concluded that it would only confuse matters if she tried to point this out.

"Hi, Henry," Pat extended her hand.

"Did you know we got married?" Susan seemed anxious to make sure Pat was up to speed.

"I saw the engagement announcement in the paper. Congratulations to you both!"

"That's kind of why we're all here today, you see."

Susan looked a little embarrassed. Pat was certainly confused. "It seems a little awkward to bring this up, but, as you may know, Henry is rather wealthy." Pat tried not to react, and said nothing. "Well, anyway, you see, Henry was getting ready to send his records to his accountant and he asked me if I had any deductions that could help offset his tax liability. Well, of course, I had all those things itemized on the computer from the stuff we got rid of. But, I told him I wouldn't feel right if I didn't pay the savings to you. Anyway, in the end, I had to tell him the whole story about Hellen, and losing my job, and not paying you. And so Henry said …"

Henry jumped in, "I told her that after everything you had done for her, and me, and the two of us, that I wanted to make sure we paid you in full." Henry handed Pat a check. "With …"

"And, you see, we really wanted to thank you in person rather than just send it in the mail," Susan interrupted.

Pat looked at the check. It was for $26,000. Before she could say anything, Henry completed his sentence, "… with interest."

To say that Pat was stunned would be an understatement. In her less-experienced days as an organizer, Pat would have objected to the interest. But now she had a firm policy never to turn down payment offered by a client. She opted to accept with a simple and genuine, "Thank you very much."

Pat was silently observing that they were three very happy people here in the kitchen, when the movers called, "We're all set. Takin' off. See ya at the big house."

"Sorry, Pat, we've got to go, you see. We need to go on ahead of the movers so we can unlock the doors for them."

"That's okay. I understand. Congratulations, again. And, again, thanks." Pat headed off toward her minivan. As she climbed in she saw Susan pull shut the front door and give it a parting pat. Henry and Susan cut across the lawn, hopped into the Porsche, and zipped off.

Pat pulled out her cell phone and pressed speed dial number two for Fred. It rang over to voicemail. "Hi, Fred. Have I got a story to tell you. Let's just say, 'we're in the money.' Tonight I'm the one who will be buying you the steak dinner – to celebrate! Call me when you can. Love you."

Pat was too wound up to go home and face her little messes. She decided to reward herself with a cup of coffee. She settled into a chair for a few quiet moments of reflection.

She had done what she knew was right. She had improved the lives of others and made peace with the satisfaction of a job well done. Then, having released the need for a material reward, she had reaped a monetary windfall. Now she sat and watched the precision system serve up beverages with the utmost efficiency, affirming on its face that the world was getting better organized. And affirming, by its continued popularity, that the world still desired more organization.

Pat savored a warm mouthful of her double mocha mud beverage, closed her eyes, and thought blissfully, confidently, that now she would write her book. Then, she opened her eyes to gaze out the window. She half expected to see a rainbow, even though the atmospheric conditions were all wrong. After all, this chapter in her life had, as her father would say, "a Hollywood ending."

Acknowledgments

I want to express my general thanks to my family, friends, colleagues, and clients who gave me the experiences from which I was able to draw for this story. But, with the gentle reminder that the book and all its characters are totally works of fiction.

Also thanks to everyone who helped in the process of selecting the book's title.

I must single out a few people for special thanks:

Shaw Mumford for her catalytic idea on character development;

Dorothy Breininger for her early and ongoing encouragement;

Standolyn Robertson for her various recommendations, business and artistic;

Renée Lane and Tiffany Voorhees of McNaughton & Gunn, Inc. for their book manufacturing expertise; and

Ed Cormany for his technical help.

And an extra special thanks to Carl for everything.